GREAT STORIES
WRITTEN BADLY

IAN WILLIAMS

First published in the United Kingdom 2018.
Copyright © Ian Williams

A catalogue record of this book is available from the British Library.
ISBN: 978-1-907463-95-2

CONTENTS

For Tiger at Baan Than Namchai
www.rotjanashands.org

FOREWORD

If you've not met Ian, you will certainly be served a generous helping of his wonderful personality in this book.

Here, he shares with you his imagination, sensitivity and the joy of telling a story, giving us characters we can all identify with on the way.

The element of nature — which can be as beautiful as it can be hostile — provides the backdrop for his stories, which Ian has developed in his own unique style.

Ultimately, as an artist and storyteller, Ian's imagination will take you into the realms of the probable, to the improbable, leaving you to decide.

Enjoy the book, and be assured that the stories within, are written by an enormously imaginative, creative and generous man.

~ Diana Mackie ~

INTRODUCTION

As a fulfilled police constable in the Thames Valley, Ian Williams could never have foreseen the blackness ahead, nor indeed the discovery of a creativity that would deliver him once again into the light. The simple act of moulding models of salt dough and the uncomplicated pleasure of baking them proved a turning point in his tumultuous life. Indeed, it was the first step in a journey which led ultimately to Skye where his working days now bring him the deepest peace.

Lan Mara, a bungalow sitting on the shore of Loch Snizort near to the capital of The Isle of Skye, with a newly constructed studio and gallery, is a far cry from Ian's life as a dog handler with the Thames Valley Police until a traumatic, violent assault left his future unclear.

Originally from Wales, Ian saw enlisting in the police force as an opportunity to help others, a guiding principle that has never left him. Nor has he ever taken the safe option — one of his first jobs as a police officer involved a suspected bomb outside of the British Museum. Having demonstrated a natural talent and passionate commitment to his work, he moved to the dog handling division and firearms tactical teams. Working with his famous dog Tyson, he represented the force at national competition level and believes the dog cage in the back of his van probably saved his life when rammed by a stolen vehicle in a high-speed chase.

A year later, Ian was maliciously attacked by a drug-crazed youth as he tried to protect another police officer. In the assault, Ian sustained such serious injuries to his arm and spinal nerves that he was invalided out of the police force after twenty years of passionate commitment to it.

Despite physical pain, post-traumatic stress and the despairing mental void into which he had been flung, Ian's naturally buoyant nature asserted itself. It was a transition assisted by his many friends, not least his wife Gill, herself a police sergeant in charge of underwater recovery, whose encouragement and sense of humour helped him find the way ahead.

Baked and painted salt dough sculptures, as a way of finding focus, led to a decision to pursue a career in fine art. At an interview, given a lump of clay, he responded with an inspired model of his own injured right hand, somehow symbolic of that fateful attack, which won him a place at Buckinghamshire University College in 1998, where he graduated with distinction. New-found skills and an unleashed creativity led him into a new world waiting outside the college walls. Over the years, Skye had already taken hold of his heart, and it was not long before Ian and Gill returned to the immense skies of Skeabost Bridge where they bought their new home. He may have spells away from the island, as with charity work for example, but for Ian, Skye has come to represent home and the door that's always open.

Now running his new artist's studio in Skeabost Bridge, Ian draws constant artistic stimulation from the world on his doorstep. A simple walk on a beach is enough to energise his creativity. Skye's landscapes and forms are reflected eloquently in his ceramics and paintings. Theses can range from confident rendering of underwater worlds where apparently boldly clashing colours form an underlying harmony, to pieces inspired by the transformation of a simple piece of driftwood or the startling geological shapes of the island. Because the seed of each individual piece lies in a past brought to life by his present, we are aware of a coherent unity to the impressive and prolific body of work of which the following pages offer but a sample.

A LETTER TO SANTA

Barbara realised that she was carrying twins at week nine. She had no idea how she was aware of this, she just knew, and she also knew that one of the twins was a girl. It was at this stage that Barbara named her daughter, Susan.

"Aggggggggh!" The staff nurse heard the blood-curdling scream from deep within the long corridor, and rushed from her station, through the swinging doorways to find Mrs. Barbara Phillips lying heavily pregnant on her bed, her face flushed red in pain. Standing next to her, her husband, Phil, was clutching her left hand.

"Er, sorry." He said, his face flushed with embarrassment, "She had a contraction, and I squeezed a bit too tight. Her hand, I mean. That made her scream."

The nurse unpeeled his vice-like grip from Barbara's hand and carried out some checks.

"All good. Please sit down Mr. Phillips. Both of you will need all your strength to see this one through. Your wife will be fine, but I'm not so sure about you." She smiled and left them.

Barbara had been admitted to hospital at seven months because from an early stage in the pregnancy doctors discovered that one of the twins was not developing in the same way as the other. There was concern, but it was unclear what the problem was. As it was her first pregnancy and she had suffered high blood pressure she had been booked in for close monitoring.

Now, only two days later, her labour had started.

Between contractions, Barbara had time to think about the events that had led to this point in her life. She recalled with the deepest of joy her skiing holiday with Phil seven months earlier in Lapland. That was when she'd first met Santa.

They had rented a traditional log cabin for ten days. Set deep within a snow-covered fell and completely surrounded by slender fir and silver birch trees, the comfortable and homely cabin had a large wood burning fireplace. After a full day of cross-country skiing, they would return to relax and sitting watching the dancing flames, the aroma and sound of burning logs had induced sleep so easily.

Included in their holiday package was an opportunity to spend two nights in a luxurious glass dome. The dome was situated some distance from the cabin and completely isolated. In the centre was a huge, and very comfortable, king size bed. Lying here gave uninterrupted views of the sky. Although these were wonderful during the day, it was at its best at night when the whole of the sky was filled with the brightest twinkling stars. It looked as though a billion diamonds were hanging just above their heads.

Now, on her hospital bed and trying hard not to be fearful, Barbara felt a glow inside her heart as she recalled her most precious memory; the beautiful intimacy she and Phil had shared and, while they were entwined in a tangle of love and affection, the sky surrounding them had burst into soft pulsing colours. Red, green, yellow and purple lights pulsed and danced to their rhythm, climaxing in an explosion of an intense aurora borealis which covered the entire sky.

In the warmth of Phil's embrace, Barbara had reached out her arms and felt her hands pass through the glass and touch the skies. She'd watched as the lights passed effortlessly through her fingers and, for a moment, her hands were glowing with the iridescent lights. She felt a rich, deep warmth in her soul, her whole body energized. Suddenly she'd taken a deep breath, and in that moment she knew she had conceived. Tears of joy trickled down her face to be gently wiped away by Phil's soft touch as he also felt the powerful emotion that had passed through his wife. Both lay in silence until contented sleep took them. As Barbara drifted away, she promised herself that at some time in the future she and her family would return to this magical place.

Another contraction, and this time it was more significant. Phil pressed the alert buzzer for the nurse. He had a look of panicked fear on his face, and the nurse took him by his hand and gently sat him on a chair, and that is where he remained for the duration of the labour.

The time had arrived, the birth was imminent.

The maternity team did their jobs gently and without a fuss. Barbara had been given drugs to assist with the pain management. In between the effort she drifted, and feeling quite calm, she simply sent herself back one more time to their visit to Lapland. This time she recalled her encounter with Santa himself.

Sitting on a huge wooden rocking chair in the centre of a large log cabin, Santa gently rocked to, and fro, he was wearing a jacket of the brightest shade of red, his boots shone like coal, and his hair and beard were brilliant white. Barbara was breathless at the sight. She had approached Santa — there were so many things she wanted to ask him but all her questions faded away as he'd smiled at her, a knowing smile that seemed to acknowledge the fact that he was aware of her future motherhood. Then he'd said, "And don't forget to write to me, Barbara. Remember your letter."

The memory suddenly vanished into a haze of pain, the vision of Santa was gone. Barbara thrashed about on the bed, aware that her body felt as though it was about to be torn in two and screamed less in pain than in surprise. The twins were born very quickly and handed to her before she could quite take in that it was all over, or rather, that it was just starting. Phil murmured, "Well done, darling. I think that one is George so this one," he stroked a tiny infant head, "must be our Susan."

The new parents were overwhelmed by the moment and were not aware of the concern that was on the midwife's face. She realised very quickly that one of the twins was much smaller than its sibling. She let the parents get on with parenthood for the time being, particularly as both Susan and George were crying heartily, and left Barbara and Phil lost in the beautiful minutes following the birth, to call in a specialist doctor.

Many tests and consultations later the family would learn of the difficulties that Susan would face. They were given probable time frames, how her condition might develop, what could be expected. The Phillips family decided that they would take each day as it presented itself and that they would make every single second count. So life went on.

From their earliest age, Barbara would whisper stories to the twins about their parent's life and experiences. In particular she often told them about the Lapland winter wonderland — the snow world — as the children would later call it. She told them about the dark skies and beautiful coloured lights and how they danced across the night sky. She told them about the wonderful glass dome and how it was as if you were outside but inside at the same time. Barbara explained the northern lights to the twins. In fact, the first words the children spoke after "mummy" and "daddy" were "aurora borealis" but it didn't always come out that way, but almost. And then Barbara would tell them about Santa and each time she thought about her visit she drifted into an almost dreamlike state. The twins listened in silence, a look of wonder on their faces, and never tired of their mother's stories.

Although they were a tightly fitting family and love flowed between them life for the Phillips was difficult. Susan was tested and re-tested for a whole array of possibilities. She was significantly smaller and physically weaker than her twin brother, but she possessed a heart and soul of steel. She was so aware of her condition and its implications, but she was a brave girl and found the courage to protect her family emotionally; a smile, a touch would sooth her parent's frustrations, and she let her brother think that it was he who was protecting her. He was her warrior, her white knight. The reality, however, was not good. Several more years passed and the doctors gave them news that they did not want to hear.

Each found a way to use up their time with Susan as best they could. Phil arranged shorter hours so he could have plenty of time at home to play with the twins and Barbara organised two days' work back at the University to give herself the task of saving enough cash to take the family to her most favourite location. She faced opposition, though. The doctors advised strongly that Susan's condition was so serious that they should not risk taking her to such extreme conditions. But Barbara had pleaded passionately that at this stage in Susan's life there was nothing to be lost, and eventually they had sanctioned the family's trip. Barbara started to draft her letter, and she would present Santa with it in person.

***

At the top of the staircase Barbara looked down on the waiting suitcases. A large, red tartan case, a smaller, bright pink case, and a small, green camouflage case. These smaller cases belonged to the twins who were now nine years old. George was tall and well-built for his age. He had a serious face — his looks were more like his father than his mother — which would light up when he did smile. The sister he constantly looked out for was much smaller, her face pale and with gaunt features. Her eyes appeared heavy and tired, and her hands were tiny and thin, but they all knew there was fire within her soul. Today, she wore a padded, pink Parka-style coat — the hood with its rim of an even brighter pink almost completely hiding her face — thick woolly tights and bright pink, fur-lined boots. She resembled a Barbie doll, the 'Winter Wonderland' range.

As Barbara watched she saw her husband dash from the living room and trip over the red case which cannoned into the pink one, setting, in turn, the green one on its side. He swore quietly, and she laughed and tutted at the same time. The twins appeared at his side, and he tidied children and cases up along one wall. He called up the stairs, "Barbara dear, the taxi is here and waiting for us."

She was half-way the down the stairs when she all but panicked as she remembered the letter which was still in her secret place in the bedroom. Rushing back up, she retrieved it and looked once more at the address, "To St. Nicholas, Lapland". She kissed it and tucked it into her jacket pocket.

"Waiting for me are you?" she sang as she skipped past her family and out to the waiting taxi.

Arriving at the terminal building, the family joined two hundred or so other travellers excited to be heading for Lapland. Christmas decorations sparkled all around the concourse, but this was nothing compared with the Lapland departure lounge. Christmas songs were playing loudly — the crowd collectively hummed along to 'Rudolf the Red-nosed Reindeer' — and a large television screen showed snow — lots of it. There were reindeer pulling sleighs, husky dogs playing in the snow and children having fun on toboggans. The excitement was tangible. Then they were called to board the aircraft. It would be just over three hours flying time to Northern Finland.

Susan, already tired by the excitement of packing and choosing what to wear, and by the airport, which was a new experience for her, fell asleep tucked between her mother and brother who had claimed the window seat. Her father, sitting across the gangway picked up the free newspaper and read the headline, "Solar Flare Will Hit Earth". Phil leaned across and said quietly to Barbara, "Did you know anything about this?"

"Hmmmm. I caught something on the radio, yesterday. What are they saying?" she replied. Phil started to read the article to her:

Scientists say that on the surface of the sun a solar flare has begun to build. It will grow so large that a bulge will be clearly visible from Earth.

"Then there's the usual bit about not looking directly at the sun," and it goes on:

The big question being asked is, 'how will it affect Planet Earth?' A twenty-four watch is being kept, and it is expected that gigantic arcs of electrical discharge will project into outer space. It is probable that power supplies and computer systems will be affected and there may be outages and reduced supplies. They expect to be able to give around twelve hours' notice of the largest events. At the moment scientists are uncertain of how extensive the impact will be. As one eminent researcher put it, 'Earth is holding her breath.'

"Well," said Phil, "at least we shall be away from everything."

Barbara squeezed Susan tightly to her side and said, "But we'll have the most spectacular northern lights."

The family were met by jolly and enthusiastic travel staff who quickly ushered them to a waiting people-carrier to begin their drive through the snowy landscape. It was only two o'clock in the afternoon, and yet the skies were a deep shade of lavender. The sun was a giant ball of muted orange against the lavender. The trees reached up to points in the sky where the snow on their tops took on this lavender tinge with an occasional hint of underlying deep green. The whole surface of the snow looked as though it was covered with tiny diamonds, sparkling and reflecting any light that touched it.

George was spell-bound by the sight of so much snow and stared at the trees as they travelled past. Then with a start, he took a sharp intake of breath and pulled back from the window, a look of surprise on his face. "George, are you okay darling?" Barbara was ever alert to her children's anxieties.

"Yes, Mummy. It's just that I thought I saw an animal or something in the trees. It looked at me."

The driver of the vehicle, hearing their conversation, spoke in a deep Finnish accent, "Don't vorry yung George, dis is jus snow creacha." And he laughed a rich, deep laugh. Checking their puzzled faces in his rear-view mirror he explained in clear English, "It is only the snow that gets too heavy for the branches then suddenly slips off. Because the snow is covered with ice, it holds its shape and can appear to be some sort of animal. Look we are almost there."

The driver indicated forward to where there were yellow lights shining in the distance. He said, "Welcome to Lapland. We hope you have a wonderful time."

Barbara looked at the driver and said to herself, "But how on earth did he know George's name?" His reflection in the rear-view mirror gave her a warm smile and Barbara could have sworn that he winked at her.

They pulled up in front of a beautifully-lit log cabin with a sign on the front that said 'Poro'. "This means 'reindeer'," their driver said as he quickly emptied his vehicle of their bags and took them in through a large wooden door. Dropping their luggage in the hallway he opened an inner door and guided the family into a room with the most beautiful smell of orange pomanders and mulled wine and with the sound of tinkling — like glass shards softly touching each other in a soft breeze. They stood in a huddle inhaling the rich aroma and realised that they were alone. The driver had tiptoed away closing the door behind him.

Barbara went and looked out through a small window in the front door to see lights vanishing into a haze of snowy mist. She thought she could hear a sound outside. Was it the tyres of the taxi as they crushed the snow-covered road surface? It sounded like a soft, *Ho, Ho, Ho!*

George, by now, had completely forgotten his brief encounter with the falling snow. Susan looked out of the big sitting room windows, her eyes wide with excitement and anticipation.

At the far end of the sitting room was an inglenook fireplace where a golden orange fire crackled and gently hissed. Barbara gathered them around the fire, which immediately warmed their faces. Susan removed her pink furry hood and smiled towards the inviting and welcoming fire. She walked in front of it and bathed her hands and face in its heat. She always felt the cold so much.

Barbara removed her coat and picked up George's from the floor where he'd abandoned it. Phil took them from her and went to hang them in the hallway while she took the children to see their bedroom. George and Susan would share a comfortable large twin-room with its own shower-room and toilet, while Barbara and Phil had an even larger en-suite room with a king-size bed.

The family quickly settled into the cabin feeling secure and content together. They cooked and ate the dinner that had been pre-stocked for them and prepared for bed. With one last look out of the windows, they could see that weather conditions were settled, the night sky was dark, clear and very cold, the stars shone brightly. Finally the tiredness of the journey sent them all to their beds.

Later, the first charged particles collided with the Earth's atmosphere. Venus cast shadows on the ground with a newly energised light. The effect was spectacular. The aurora borealis shimmied across the horizon, ribbons of light crossing the night sky followed by bright pulses of emerald green lights that were joined by brilliant crimson, yellow, blue and purple curtains swishing and folding across the darkness. The lights danced, coming into focus then out, pulse after pulse spreading across the vastness.

As the sky filled with coloured lights, the lower atmosphere seemed to crackle with electricity as particles gently flowed down, lower and lower. They landed softly on the highest fells then touched the highest tree tops, falling like invisible snow all around, slowly but surely landing on the rooftops of all of the buildings and finally down onto the ground.

In a snow-covered clearing, several sapling fir trees stood together forming a circle. Towering over them, as majestic as can be, was a large Honga Tree — the Honga Tree is revered and held sacred within the Arctic Circle. Covered in thick snow, its boughs stretched out as if caressed. Its wooden limbs awakened from a long sleep, reaching far they embraced the refreshing life force.

As the charged particles covered the saplings, the tallest shook what appeared to be a large pointed hat, and the others joined in. The trees became animated, just like a group of small wizard-like people huddled together, communicating. They were waiting for their instructions from the Honga Tree.

Iridescent coloured light danced all around the great Honga Tree, and the saplings began to attach themselves to it forming a swaying clump of fir trees. A large mound of snow suddenly twitched and shuddered, growing and shape-shifting into a form. Becoming larger and larger, a great white snow bear stood tall, shook its entire body and immediately glowed with the same coloured light. Half the size of the Honga Tree nonetheless it towered over the saplings, its eyes glowing with the same life-creating particles. Other familiar creatures appeared from the snow — wolves, cats and even, pigs. All of these creatures had waited a very long time to be re-energised and waited, glowing in front of the Honga Tree where they were to be given their tasks. For the Honga Tree, it was a long-awaited moment for his friends to come together and carry out his plans.

Unaware of the auroral activity outside, Barbara and Phil drifted into a deep, comfortable and welcome sleep. The day had been long, and they were so happy to be on holiday with their children. The stress of recent times had all but exhausted them, particularly Barbara, but now her dream was actually happening — she was in Lapland with her family. She settled into a deep slumber knowing that Susan and George were fast asleep in their own comfortable pine beds in the other room.

As they all slept, coloured lights from outside of the cabin started to dance against the window panes reflecting off the fine ice crystals that hung in the air. Now they flooded the interior of the cabin with multi-coloured shades of light, passing through both the glass and timber. The fire in the inglenook fireplace flickered into life, golden flames licking upwards, swaying and dancing in the hearth, seeming to acknowledge the arrival of the aurora. The ice crystals floated around the cabin creating subtle musical sounds as they moved.

While the music played, the ice crystals started to group together, each individual crystal fitting perfectly to the next one, slowly gathering together to make a form. The light emanating from the form intensified, details became clearer — a head and shoulders, followed by a torso and legs — though there were no clear facial features. No more than the size of a large child, the light entity floated just above the floor, moving elegantly, gently swaying to the beautiful music. It approached the parent's bedroom, passing effortlessly through the closed doorway and into where Barbara and Phil slept soundly and peacefully. Moving silently, it approached Barbara's side of the bed and lowered its head towards her face. Barbara stirred and raised her head from the soft pillow. There was no sense of surprise on her face as she came to and, silently uncovering herself, got out of bed leaving Phil completely unaware, his breathing easy and contented.

The light entity offered Barbara a small illuminated hand, which she took into her own, and she was immediately aware of floating up from the bedroom floor. Her body was enrobed in ice-crystal light and, with a look of wonder on her face, she levitated hand-in-hand with the entity, towards the bedroom door. Without opening it, they passed through into the lounge where they paused to watch the coloured lights. Barbara's face gleamed with delight, and she put out her free hand and caressed the streaming ice crystals. Several landed on her palm where they transformed into warm orange and golden flames that swayed to and fro before floating towards the hearth where they coalesced with the fire.

Barbara began to laugh as she took in all of this magical activity. Then her attention was focused towards the doorway to her daughter's room where Susan was standing, barefoot. Barbara called out, "Susan what are you doing out of bed so late?" It was an interesting remark considering that Susan's mummy was floating above the floor and no sound had actually left her lips. Then, she heard a sort of familiar voice in her mind, "Susan cannot see nor hear you, Barbara."

"But what is she doing? She should be sleeping?"

"Oh, but she is Barbara, she is. Follow me."

Still holding hands the entity, Barbara floated across the lounge, and as they did so, Susan walked forwards underneath them towards the front door. Barbara looked into the bedroom and saw the small form of her poorly daughter, apparently still asleep in her bed, her brother George across the room also asleep in his own bed.

Barbara looked again at her daughter as she approached the now open outside door and, with a gasp, she realised that Susan was going to go outside into the freezing cold. The entity gave her hand a reassuring squeeze.

As Barbara watched Susan cross the threshold, she could see that there was something in her tiny right hand and knew immediately that it was the sealed letter addressed to St. Nicholas.

Dear Saint Nicholas. Please, please hear me. My beloved Susan is so poorly; my only wish is for her to get better. The thought of losing her is just too terrible to comprehend. Please, please for pity sake let her stay with us. She is only a baby, our little baby. I plead with you, I have always believed in you, a gift for Susan is all I want. I have been a good and loving mother to both my children, for God's sake do something, please do something. Please hear me. Barbara

Susan walked outside into the night.

An overwhelming wave of emotion almost crushed Barbara, and huge tears fell from her eyes. As they rolled down her cheeks, her companion caught them all in her glowing hand. Closing the hand for several seconds, the entity revealed a single sparkling teardrop-shaped crystal gemstone in her palm. She offered this to Barbara who heard that strangely familiar voice in her head saying, "This is yours, a memory, a gift."

Barbara accepted the gem without question and put it into her pyjama trouser pocket. The sadness passed completely.

Through the doorway, Barbara could see several low-growing shrubs, covered in a shimmering snow, which began to change shape before her eyes. Blurred at first, the many tiny globes of multicoloured snow crystals covering each shrub seemed to spark the movement. Graceful white hooves emerged from the soft fresh-fallen snow. Where there was a shrub a moment ago, now stood a beautiful snow pony, its eyes sparkling like tiny diamonds, twinkling with life and energy. It turned slightly and bowed its head towards Susan and, with a whinny, swished its mane and tail making a sound like a thousand tiny violins played together as one. Behind the pony, another shape began to emerge. This time a small crystal trap was revealed with a sapling driver who was wearing a pointed hat. The driver nodded towards Susan and indicated for her to sit up alongside. Barbara could only look on in amazement.

Susan walked calmly towards the pony and trap, each step she took on the freezing snow producing aurora lights around her feet, seeming to shroud them and make it look as if she was wearing crystal shoes. She skipped directly toward the steps and glided onto the seat next to her driver. A look of pure delight and happiness covered her small white face. The illuminated lights that were hanging in the air then settled all over her and were absorbed into her body. She began to glow with all the colours of a wonderful aurora, and she started to laugh a little girl's pure giggly laugh.

Above, Barbara floated with her companion, in awe and wonderment at the scene unfolding below.

With another swish of its silver-white mane, the pony's musical whinny intensified and it raised its head. The driver took up the silvery reins and pulled back. The pony and trap began to move, slowly at first but with every step, lights sprang from the underside of its hooves, and as it gained speed it lifted lightly up into the air. As it moved higher, sparkles and shimmering lights engulfed them and, as they moved forwards, snow-covered fir trees moved aside tipping their hats towards their visitors, creating an avenue of lights through which the pony and riders travelled. With every stride forward, more and more snow creatures shimmered and appeared from the dormant mounds of snow that lay all around. Each creature was suffused with the light of the aurora borealis. Each creature nodded its head as Susan and the pony and trap passed by. Susan giggled with joy, her companion leaping up and down on the seat, silver reins in hand as their journey continued towards a more intense source of light. In the distance was a large dome, its huge shape a mass of ice crystals holding themselves together like gigantic, pearlised soap bubbles built up from the ground.

Barbara and her companion followed at a comfortable speed with seemingly no effort at all. They flew just above the ground where Barbara could feel the breeze in her hair and on her face. She thought she should at least have lifted a scarf from the clothes pegs by the door as they'd left the cabin, but strangely it wasn't the freezing cold she'd expected, it was, if anything, warm! It all felt real but very unreal all at the same time.

Ahead, Barbara could see the dome but no sign of her daughter. A brief sense of concern threatened to crush her once more but was quickly dismissed with a responding thought from her companion, "Susan arrived long before us. She is quite safe." Barbara once again thought that she recognised the voice in her head but still could not place it.

As they approached the wall of the dome, a section shimmered and became a small archway through which Barbara and her companion glided with ease. When Barbara turned to look back at the archway, it had disappeared. Her eyes were wide with wonder at the interior of the dome, a thrilling sensation coursed through her body and she instinctively knew she was in a safe and loving space. They settled themselves on a high sofa as though they were in a box at the theatre.

Inside the bubble dome, which was very much larger on the inside than the outside, there was a great many activities going on but the only sounds came from ice crystals moving against one another creating a soft, rhythmic ticking song, accompanied by a subtle humming from various flying creatures — haw frost insects, large snow owls, even several flying penguins all softly flapping their wings. As they flapped they shed fresh ice crystals which found their way to the chandeliers and joined the flames that burned there. The huge crystal chandeliers floated unattached in the air, their orange and golden flames dancing with the music, like ballroom dancers gliding delicately on a grand ballroom floor.

In the centre of the dome, the Honga Tree swayed as a musical director would, conducting his orchestra. The Tree was communicating with all of the creatures by using thought. This worked very well, and there was no confusion as to any of the requests being made and any of the tasks getting done. Everyone got on with what they had to do. There was a sense of excitement within the dome, which intensified as the Honga Tree stood erect and turned about, its strong limbs almost coming to attention. This brought complete silence and stillness within the dome.

Slowly, the bubble dome itself started to shimmer and the light inside intensified. The flames in the chandeliers became richer and more golden; ice crystals creating the walls of the dome in front of the Honga tree separated and re-formed into a beautiful archway; all of the saplings moved to either side of the opening and formed an avenue; snow creatures presented themselves in line — the smaller creatures — several mice, rats, and chinchillas — were followed by small bears, then several snow dogs and cats, snow pot-bellied pigs and sheep — to form a proud guard of honour. The avenue led directly to the Honga Tree who stood strong and majestic in the centre of the dome. The Tree was flanked on both sides by the most beautiful, giant snow tigers who stood with their heads held high, just high enough for the Honga Tree to pat them. The tigers purred with delight.

Soft music started to play once again, this time with the sound of bells and the fine hum of song bowls. The sudden sound of a whinny announced the arrival, then, of the small snow pony and trap together with its guest of honour. They entered through the arch and, as they came to a silent stop within the dome, ice crystals appeared to explode just like fireworks in their wake. What an entrance!

Susan giggled with delight at all that she could see in front of her, slipped from her seat and floated to the ground. As her tiny feet made contact with the snow, floor lights surrounded her. Clutching the letter, she skipped between the assembled creatures and headed straight towards the Honga Tree. As she passed along the avenue of snow creatures, they all nodded their heads each releasing tiny iridescent globes of light that floated toward her. Her little body absorbed each one, and she started to glow with every colour within the dome.

As Susan approached the Honga Tree, it shimmered and shape-shifted. The light blurred and cleared to reveal a large, well-built man wearing a red jacket with pure white fur around the rim, so much like Susan's pink parka coat. The man wore brilliantly shiny black boots and had the fullest sparkling white beard.

Susan ran the last couple of steps and launched herself into the waiting arms of Santa Claus. Scooping her up he pulled her close, a smile came to his face, and he kissed her tiny forehead. The atmosphere within the dome erupted into a sound of pure joy. The animals danced with the saplings and the tigers purred with complete satisfaction. Barbara looked down, transfixed and knew that tears were not far away.

Susan pushed the letter into Santa's gloved hand, giggled, then wriggled out of his gentle grip. She hugged the tigers making them purr even louder and skipped away to be immediately surrounded by all of the snow creatures, all wanting to hug her and send their light globes into her. Susan played games with the smaller saplings — a game of hide and seek — Susan was very good at finding them, but they were not so good at locating her.

Barbara watched her daughter at the far side of the dome. A brief giggle interrupted her thoughts. The sound was so familiar to her, but she simply could not place it. Susan was running as fast as she could in and out of the sapling trees, which were swishing to all sides attempting to follow her as she ran. Every time Susan brushed against the saplings more and more ice crystals floated and gently landed on her. Her cheeks were flushed with fresh pink, and her eyes shone brightly as she played. A flying snow penguin swooped down from high in the air and picked her up with its enormous white flippers. Susan sat comfortably within them as she was carried higher and higher up into the dome, the sound of her laughter so infectious that all of the snow creatures looked up to enjoy the moment.

Barbara looked on in wonder. She could not believe that her sick little girl appeared so healthy and well. She had never seen her able to enjoy life like this, had never seen her run so fast, never seen such richness of colour in her face, nor heard the sound of her laughter. Barbara then recalled her message to St. Nicholas and thought to herself, "Could it be, is she cured, did I do enough?"

In her mind, Barbara heard a reply to her thought question. She turned to her left and standing next to her was the figure of a large man. He had a white beard and bright sparkling eyes. He was dressed in a simple off-white robe. Barbara smiled at him, and he returned a warm, affectionate smile. At the same time she heard in her mind, "Barbara you have been a very good mother to both Susan and George. Now it is time to leave."

"But I've only just arrived. I want to continue watching Susan enjoying herself. Please, I never want this to end!"

"It is time to leave," said the voice in her mind, "Barbara, it's time to leave."

The voice was soft and familiar, "Barbara, my love, it's time to go."

Opening her eyes, light poured in, and Barbara felt unsure of herself. A warm hand still held hers, but it was no longer the light entity guiding her. She heard her husband nearby.

"Barbara, the cars are waiting. We're all waiting for you, love. It's time to go."

Susan's funeral was so sad, a nine year old girl who was given such little time, laid to rest.

The weeks passed by. There was a tangible sadness in the house, but there was also something else, a quiet comfort, that life must, and always does, go on.

Barbara returned, still part-time, to her job as a researcher. Phil continued his work as a forestry manager, and George returned to school. His friends were very kind to him and encouraged him to continue with his sports. He was exceptional at rugby, his size and strength giving him an advantage on the field. The family tried to get on with their lives as normal, but it was tough. Susan had dominated their time, not that any of them had resented this. In fact, they had relished her company because although she was physically weak, she possessed such great strength in other areas. In her touch, her smile and her eyes, she could melt the hardest of hearts and regularly did.

One bright Sunday morning as they were sitting around the breakfast table, George seemed to be miles away in thought. In his hand was a tiny object that he passed from one finger to another. It caught the sunlight from outside, and a shaft of brilliantly coloured light hit a mirror on the opposite wall to where he was sitting. This light then reflected around the room, which made Barbara look up. She asked in a soft tone, "What is that George?" Opening his hand she saw, sitting comfortably within his palm, a beautiful crystal conker. Barbara was slightly taken aback, "Where did that come from, my love?"

George began, "We were playing together. Susan was running so much faster than me, then I couldn't find her when we played 'hide and seek' but she gave me hints, and I found her hiding up an old dead-looking tree. I could hardly see her on the branch, she seemed to be part of it, and she looked like she was surrounded with coloured lights. So, when we finished playing, we walked around for a while and she told me that she loved me but the thing was, Susan didn't speak. It was weird; I could just hear what she said in my head. We found some big conkers and started to play. Of course, Susan won, and my conker smashed into pieces onto the ground, but I wasn't disappointed. I was happy that Susan had won. I was surprised when she bent down and picked up the pieces, though, because when she handed them to me, it was like this! I thought I must have been dreaming all of it until the morning of her funeral when I found the conker in my pocket. It did happen, I know it must have happened Mummy, it must have!"

Huge tears flowed down George's red cheeks, and Phil leaned over and drew his head into his arms and said, "George, don't upset yourself, the same happened to me. Susan and I wandered through the forest together; you know how she would love us to push her chair around the trees. This time she felt strong enough to walk, and she held my hand. I could feel her warmth but more than that I could feel her strength, and we talked, we talked about so many things, but just like you described, the words were in our minds, we didn't speak out loud. She also seemed to be slightly older, but I couldn't understand how that was or how old she was. Then we began to gather pine cones, like we all have over the years. You remember how we would spray them silver and gold and make Christmas decorations. It was strange, Susan put the words 'I love you Dad' into my mind. The last thing I recall was her surrounded by bright coloured lights — in fact, she seemed to be made of the lights! When we got back home from the service, I changed my clothes, and in my trousers pocket I found this."

Phil produced a beautiful crystal fir cone which he placed on the table in front of him. George added his crystal conker and

Barbara opened her palm to reveal a teardrop-shaped crystal. She told them her story, and while telling it, the crystal items aligned themselves into the centre of the table. Suddenly sunlight shone through the window onto the crystals, iridescent light refracting through them, filling the room. This light began to take form as it hovered in the space where Susan would have sat. The form was pure light, and with outstretched arms, the form touched her family. The three of them saw Susan in that light, her smiling face looking directly at each of them bringing a calm silence.

A look of wonder filled their eyes, brief tears of joy fell down their cheeks, and the family reached out and held each other's outstretched hands. In that moment each heard in their mind a familiar voice. Susan said, "Yes, all done. I love you all." Then as her shape began to vanish they all heard her giggling, a rich giggle before she added in a whisper that became quieter, "I am so very happy now. I will never leave you, just look into the crystals." Then Susan was gone.

DRIFTWOOD

The journey north-west from Cheshire took longer than anticipated; road works on the M6 motorway, then diversions entering Scotland. Eventually, Tom and Elly approached their holiday destination, a small island on the coast, west of Glasgow.

The Isle of Great Cumbrae nestles in the River Clyde, in between Largs on the mainland and the beautiful Isle of Bute.

The last ferry which would take them across the short span of the Clyde was ready to leave. They had made it to Largs just in time. As Tom drove their VW estate straight on board, he felt as if he was being watched and judged by the other passengers for being 'that last minute car'. He thought to himself, "At least we didn't miss the crossing, holidays here we come, to hell with what they think!"

It seemed that even before the doors of the ferry were set closed that it was on its way crossing the estuary of the Clyde to the slipway on Great Cumbrae.

Molly, affectionately known as Mol, had whined for the last hour, clearly wanting a pee. However, with the timing for the last ferry as tight as it was, frustratingly she'd had to wait — no real issue for the four-year old tri-coloured springer spaniel; she simply liked to whinge.

Last on first off the ferry, well how tough was that! Tom drove and turned left, stopping a little way along the narrow lane to let the other traffic pass before he opened the rear of the car. When he did, Mol came flying out, panting and looking in all and every direction, her tail wagging furiously. Rabbits! There must be rabbits. Then, oh! Perhaps a pee. She squatted for what seemed like ten minutes.

Tom said, "Come on Mol, we haven't got all day." Mol slowly but surely approached the car until she thought she saw another rabbit, a little dart here and there, always with one eye on Tom. Then at her own pace, she walked to the back of the car and jumped in, sitting and looking directly into Tom's face. Elly, from the front of the car, said, "Good girl! Did you catch those pesky rabbits?"

Tom got back in and drove south along the lane, their final destination the west coast. Even though it was approaching ten o'clock, there was still enough light to show them the beautiful and inspiring location. At the same moment, both Tom and Elly exclaimed in an exhalation of excitement, "Wow!"

Sitting almost on the shore was 'Driftwood', a single storey croft cottage with a red tin roof and white-washed walls. The base of the walls sitting on a solid rock base, the building seemed to grow organically from the bedrock. There were two tiny windows to the rear of the cottage overlooking the wild uncluttered views up the hills. There was only one other building visible from these windows and sitting on top of a hill it must have panoramic views of the whole island. At the front was a beautiful ultramarine blue door and another two small windows overlooking the seashore and, in the distance, the Isle of Bute. From the front door, they could see the shoreline where gentle waves washed over pebbles of all sizes and colours and the sound of the water was soothing and fresh. In the distance to the north-west remnants of the sunset were quickly fading.

The setting was perfect; the evening was perfect, all was well.

Parking the car, Elly said, "Let's unpack in the morning, shame to miss the end of this sunset. I'll get the bubbles."

Elly fished around and produced a bottle of bubbly. Quickly finding two tin mugs from the kitchen, she joined Tom who was stretching his tired back and watching Mol running and darting about on the shore, chasing the oystercatchers who were attempting to sleep on the pebbles.

Tom and Elly walked to several larger boulders and sat down before Elly popped the cork and decanted the bubbly into the tin mugs. Tom said, "Strange how good bubbles taste out of an old tin mug!" Elly agreed and took a deep thirst quenching drink. Immediately the effects hit both of them, and they began to giggle while Mol darted about in hysterical doggy excitement, running at high speed, doing an impeccable handbrake turn and galloping back to where she'd started, all of the time keeping one eye on her best friends who were in hysterics a few metres away.

Tiredness from the journey and the wonderful tin mug bubbles took effect on both of them. They entered the cottage and found the bedroom. The interior of the room was illuminated by a small table lamp, and a tall bed was made up ready with sheets, several blankets, and a thick eiderdown. Tom and Elly stripped off and launched themselves into the welcoming bed. They held each other tightly and kissed. Then, without warning, the door slammed open, and Mol jumped onto the bed landing in the middle of them. This they met with hysterical laughter.

When the laughter had settled, Elly said, "We were so lucky to get this place at such short notice." Tom replied, "Yes, I was told that it was a last minute cancellation, or something like that. Anyway, Mol has decided that we are going to sleep. I love you, night-night." Tom turned onto his side and fell into a deep sleep almost immediately. Elly lay on her back looking into space. She was happy, very happy. She was with the two most important people in her life, Tom and of course Mol. Thinking about getting into the water in the morning, she wondered what surprises they could look forward to. They had never dived in this part of the country, but they had researched what to expect. She fell asleep visualising what they might encounter. In the stillness of the night, the only sounds were that of the silence, and the soothing movement of the sea gently rolling in and out over the pebbles with a regular rhythm almost rocking tired travellers in their sleep.

Mol suddenly began to growl deeply, quietly at first and then the growling intensified. She pushed herself further in between the sleeping couple and continued to growl. Elly stirred and in a half-sleep patted Mol and said, "There, there Mol, go to sleep." But Mol did not go to sleep, she continued to growl, then she snapped her teeth together very hard making a spitting sound. Elly stirred again and sat bolt upright at the sound. In the three-quarter darkness, she looked past Mol and, with a sharp intake of breath, called out.

Against the back wall, in the shadows, Elly saw features of a young man. He had short blond hair, was clean shaven and he was staring back at Elly. Even in the dullness, she could see his blue eyes. Mol barked a blood curdling bark. Elly looked down at her and then back to the spot in the corner. There was nothing there. She blinked and refocused, still nothing. Mol had stopped growling, but now she was on Elly's pillow.

Elly shook Tom saying, "Wake up Tom, wake up!" Tom stirred and muttered something unintelligible. Elly punched him on the upper arm. "Tom, wake up now!" This was a command, and instantly Tom was wide awake but completely disoriented. "What, what is it?" he asked.

Elly said, "Someone was standing over there."

"What? Where?" Tom sat up straight and looked into the corner of the room, "I can't see anything, are you sure?" He should have known better than to have uttered the words, "Yes! Of course, I'm sure. Even Mol saw something; she woke me up with her growling."

Tom, now fully awake, looked more closely into the area

Elly had indicated. He could see shifting mottled images and looking for the source he realised that the curtains gently moving in the light breeze and the light being cast by the moon, which was still bright in the night sky, was causing a shimmering movement in that area.

Turning to Elly, he said, "It was just the shadow caused by the curtains and the moonlight."

Elly replied, "But it was so real and what about Mol?"

Tom said, "Well it was a long day for Mol as well as us, let's get some more sleep."

Realising that she was making a mountain out of a molehill, Elly softly stroked Mol on her head, Mol responding with a grumbling sound which Elly knew was contentment. Elly turned onto her side and looked at Tom who was gently breathing, the sound soon putting her back into a comfortable and reassured slumber.

They all woke several hours later in the usual manner. This meant that the first person to stir, Elly, was pounced on by Mol, a huge dog paw clouting her on the chest, followed by lots of face licking. Then Tom stirred and received the same treatment.

Following a leisurely breakfast, they unloaded the car of all of their scuba diving equipment: cylinders, dive suits, fins, weights and all of the rest of the kit they'd need. The Clyde Estuary has many interesting things to investigate including ship wrecks but Tom and Elly simply wanted to enjoy a couple of shallow shore dives, search for fish, enjoy the wealth of amazing colours to be found in soft corals, rocks and plants, or even swim with the seals, and even better, encounter dolphins.

It was a simple task to get ready to dive from the comfort of the cottage with an easy entrance into the water via a sandy pathway that had been cleared of stones and pebbles. Mol was safely shut indoors while Elly and Tom got ready for the first dive. Both were skilled divers and took no risks. Carefully they checked each other's equipment before entering the water and once they did another check for any leaks. They were both fine and so with the sign meaning 'ready and happy', they vented the air from their stab jackets and slowly descended, blending into the clear water.

Once underwater they signalled they were happy to continue and they began to fin forward.

Watching how the sunlight penetrates the water and reflects off the seabed was always a highlight for Tom and Elly; the light appears like trumpets pointing down through the water, fish dance through the shafts of light, sea kelp sways to and fro in the gentle movement of the water. They continued into deeper water, then levelled the depth out at fifteen metres. Diving close to each other, Tom took Elly's hand, and they finned through the water as one, listening to the gentle, cracking sounds coming from the seabed and watching the sub-aqua dancing of the fish and the sea kelp. Here, Tom and Elly were totally at peace with nature and each other. Nothing could spoil this special moment for them.

After ten minutes Elly checked the air contents on her equipment, she had about sixty minutes remaining. Tom indicated that he had about fifty minutes of air left so, they were about to turn around and head back when something caught Tom's eye; Elly saw it too.

Ahead of them were very fine bubbles that appeared to be coming up from a deeper point beneath them but something was not quite right, and at that moment they were surrounded by the bubbles.

Elly very quickly became disoriented as the bubbles were going both up and down. She realised that they had been drawn into a sea vortex, a whirlpool. She looked around but couldn't see Tom. She checked her depth gauge, and it told her she was now thirty metres! Elly immediately pressed her stab jacket inflation valve, but still, she sank; she started to fin heavily but still sank, and the display reading was now forty metres. A brief feeling of panic hit her, and she doubled her finning in an effort to escape the down pull. Her breathing became heavy with the effort and, checking the air contents in her cylinder, to her horror it was down to only fifteen minutes. Elly gathered herself and focused her mind.

"Panic will kill me," she thought to herself. "Calm down, calm down."

In calming herself down, she realised that the down current had stopped and she was beginning to ascend. She looked up and saw the sunlight penetrating the surface; that was where she was going to go, and it felt good.

As she kicked, she felt her fins snagging, almost as if her leg was pulled down harshly and she was somehow tangled in something. She felt pressure on her stab jacket as though she had been punched. Elly pulled and finned with all her strength, panic returning, her breathing intensified, the sound of air filling her stab jacket screaming. She looked down, and in the darker water, she thought she saw a hand disappearing into the deeper water. The hand was sinking quickly past her knee then her fins. What she saw next increased her breathing even more.

A shaft of sunlight penetrated the water and hit metal. Elly saw that an aeroplane tail section with what appeared to be an 'Iron Cross' painted on it. "What the fuck!" Elly screamed to herself, a wave of terror engulfed her. She had to focus to rationalise, but panic was squeezing her senses.

With all her effort Elly finned again and freed herself. Still, in panic she was gripping her air fill valve, her stab jacket was full, and air was escaping from the dump valves. With this amount of air in her jacket, she began to ascend too quickly, the compressed air in her lungs expanding and being forced out. Elly was in agony. Ascending out of control she lost consciousness.

Hovering in neutral buoyancy, Tom was floating at ten metres.

He'd seen the bubbles and then lost sight of Elly; his training told him to stay put and observe. He witnessed Elly descending very quickly, surrounded by bubbles and Tom realised that she had been caught in a spontaneous mini whirlpool. He waited and continued looking into the deep water. He then heard the sound of escaping air and concentrated on where the bubbles had vanished. Tom immediately realised that Elly was ascending like a cork. He said to himself, "Too fast, Elly, dump your air, dump your air!"

Elly was travelling upwards at speed, Tom gathered himself and went into action.

As she approached him, he grabbed her emergency air dump valve pulling as hard as he could, at the same time finning as fast as he could downwards to slow Elly's ascent. He knew that at this rate Elly could easily tear open her lungs, as the air she had taken in under pressure was expanding at an alarming rate, and that could kill her.

Tom held onto Elly and slowed her ascent, stopping at five metres depth. At this point Elly regained consciousness. She looked into Tom's eyes, and he saw abject terror. Tom squeezed Elly's arms, he shouted through his demand valve, "Elly, Elly, you are safe, look at me, you are safe!" Even though the words were muffled, Elly could hear it was Tom's voice. As his words began to register in her mind, she began to calm herself, and she started to draw on her experience. Slowly she gathered herself, slowing her breathing rate while Tom held on tight not dropping eye contact. They had both trained extensively over the years; Elly was qualified as a 'Dive Leader' while Tom was trained up to 'Advanced Diver'. Between them, they had clocked in excess of three hundred dive hours. Elly had always trusted Tom's diving skills and felt completely safe as his 'dive buddy', and so she began to control her feelings. Tom calmly indicated to her that they needed to go a little deeper and indicated his depth gauge. It sunk in and Elly gave the 'ok' sign. He drew her slowly down to ten metres and stayed there for ten minutes while decompressing, sharing his mouthpiece with her. At least now she was safe.

Tom and Elly swam to the shore where they quickly took off their equipment and dumped it outside. Mol flew out of the cottage going straight to Elly and looked at her with an enquiring stare. They all then got into the car and travelled a short distance to the local medical centre. Luckily, the Doctor specialised in diving related problems.

Running through the sequence of events, Dr. Ross asked Elly, "I see that you are still wearing your dive computer, may I have a look at it?" Elly took the diver's computer off her wrist and said, "In the rush to get here I forgot to take it off," and handed it to Dr. Ross. He examined the unit then plugged in a USB connection to his laptop.

He said, "You're in luck, I've just returned from a medical diving conference in Aberdeen. We were given the latest programmes for investigating diving accidents. I only installed my copy yesterday, so here we go."

The laptop started to work; quiet bleeps came from the unit, then Dr. Ross said, "Are you sure your maximum depth was forty metres?" Elly replied, "Yes, quite sure."

"Your computer profile tells me that your maximum depth was only fifteen metres, your intake of air did peak for about one minute, then returned to normal. Let's go over the details again, shall we?"

Elly and Tom explained the circumstances once more.

Dr. Ross said, "During my investigations into diving incidents I can only recall one similar recorded event. It concerned a dive group in a location called the 'Zanussi Run'. Basically, the divers went into a whirlpool, surrounded by bubbles as you were, but one dive profile did not record the maximum depth, it only recorded the depth at which the diver entered the vortex. The diver maintained that he went much deeper. However with no other evidence no more came of it.

"I've often wondered if when you enter a whirlpool, and it would depend on the size of the bubbles, but it seems to me that if the bubbles are small enough and in such quantities, they might act as some sort of shield. You could go deeper without the effects of the water pressure on your body.

"I think, Elly, that you have experienced this anomaly and have got away without serious damage."

Dr. Ross conducted a thorough examination of Elly taking blood samples and testing them on site using the latest diving related equipment. At the end of a two-hour consultation, Dr. Ross said, "You have been extremely fortunate. Your blood shows no signs of micro bubbles, in fact, it is the best sample of blood I have ever seen, your lung function is perfect as is your brain function. You are as fit as a flea, now go away and enjoy the rest of your holiday."

He said, the last few words with a huge grin on his rugged face.

Tom and Elly returned to the cottage. Mol was so relieved to be able to play on the shore, running around and around. Elly was feeling a little reflective as she considered what had taken place during the earlier dive. She shuddered at the vision of the white hand beneath her and wondered about the tail section with the markings. Of course, she hadn't mentioned this during her consultation, "God! It was bad enough as it was," she said out loud to herself. Tom looked out from the cottage. "Did you call Darling?" Elly said, "No, just talking out loud to myself."

Elly's thinking time was brought to an abrupt end as Mol pounced on her with soaking paws, licking her face. She attempted to push Mol off, but she was having none of it; Mol pawed and licked Elly as though she had not seen her for ages. Elly was in hysterics laughing and rolling about on the ground. Tom came out doors to see what all of the fuss was about and was then attacked in the same joyful way by Mol. All three played for the next few minutes, and when the hilarities had subsided Tom said, "Shall we get dinner in the local Inn, I think it's called the 'Kyles of Bute'; the menu looked great." Elly agreed.

The 'Kyles of Bute', or as the locals called it, 'The Bute', was a long, single-storey building, white-washed, and with several tiny windows to the front which overlooked the sea and the Isle of Bute. There was only one entrance which took Elly and Tom straight into the bar.

Standing at the bar were several men: two wore green boiler suits with yellow wellies, the others wore tweed jackets. It was difficult to put an age on any of them as they all had weathered faces: either crofters or fishermen, thought Tom. They were all talking together but as soon as the new arrivals walked in, all chatting stopped, and an uneasy silence ensued. The silence was broken by the barman who was younger and had a twinkle in his bright blue eyes. "Good evening folks, can I help you?" he said, in a pleasant, soft Scottish tone. Tom said, "Are you serving food tonight?"

The barman replied, "Why yes we are. Come, take a seat in the window and I'll fetch you a menu."

One of the older men at the bar said, without looking in their direction, "So you'll be stayin' at the 'Driftwood' then. They say folks don't stay there for long, too scared, you know." The barman quickly butted in, "Donald! Stop! These are our guests; you will show respect!" He stepped out from behind the bar with two menus, approaching Elly and Tom and said, in a voice that could be clearly heard from the group of men, "Teck nay notice, he's an ole fool." He winked as he reassured them. Elly said, "How does he know where we are staying?"

The barman said, "It's the way it is. Your business is their business!" Again he said, it with a smile and wink.

Tom and Elly began to laugh, the emotion and excitement of the day catching up with them, the men at the bar joining in.

The evening meal went off without any further interruptions, and they left feeling content.

Arriving back at the cottage both Elly and Tom received a huge and licky welcome from Mol. She was let out for her night-time pee, running round and round until, exhausted, she trotted back to the cottage door, drooling and covered in seaweed, where she sat waiting for her evening meal.

Tom lit the small coal fire and poured a couple of drams.

The couple sat on a soft, thick sheepskin rug with their backs against the sofa. Mol was sprawled out right in front of the fire, steam rising from her damp coat. Every few minutes she would open an eye to check that all was well.

Sipping her dram, Elly said, "What do you think that old boy meant when he said that folks are too scared to stay here?"

Tom replied, "Who knows what an old codger like that will say — it's probably his standing joke, I mean, we are quite remote here and, well, I suppose he thinks every visitor is from some big city and that they can't deal with the isolation or maybe he simply had one too many?"

Elly said, "I really like this place. I know we've only been here for a couple of days, but it feels so welcoming and homely." She sipped her dram again, and Mol stretched and groaned as if to say, 'Yeh, yeh. Keep the noise down; I'm trying to sleep!'

The heat from glowing embers in the fire touched their faces; sleep was approaching the pair. They sat in front of the fire for a few more minutes then went to bed. Of course, they were closely followed by Mol. Taking her place on her bed, Mol occupied the centre third of what she saw as her bed, which she had allowed her friends to share. Mol immediately fell into a deep sleep, twitching, and snorting as in her doggy dreams she was chasing those pesky rabbits and nearly caught one. Tom and Elly were unaware of the chase for they had fallen into a deep and welcome sleep, themselves.

Elly woke up suddenly. She was entering the water, which was warm, but she was fully clothed!

Walking deeper into the water, she was moving under the water, her vision was clear, and she could see many details: coloured fish swimming along, golden seaweed swaying as if hearing music being played, sunlight shimmering through the surface into the depths.

Then in front of her from out of a blurring, an aircraft came into view. It was intact almost and gleaming new, and she could see the wings and the tail section. Clearly visible on the tail section was the 'Iron Cross'.

Seated within the cockpit at the aircraft controls was a young blond-haired man who was not wearing a uniform but casual clothing. He smiled at Elly.

Elly continued to look at the scene as if from outside a goldfish bowl, but she was also in the scene.

She could not make sense of what she was seeing until recognition struck her. She recognised the man in the cockpit. She had seen him briefly once before!

Elly tried to speak. "Who are you?" But no words came. She tried again, "Who are you?" Nothing.

Then the blond, young man smiled at her and mouthed a word. Elly tried to make sense of it and said, "I can't understand what you're trying to say, I'm sorry." A kindly frustration appeared on the man's features, and again he smiled at Elly.

The beams of sunlight penetrating the water created patterns around the whole vision. As fish crossed the shafts of light they briefly became luminous silver; the sea-kelp turned into golden ribbons.

Then Elly watched as the pilot put a hand up to his chest pocket. He was holding a glass vial which he put into his pocket. Then he pointed at Elly and patted his chest pocket. Again he pointed his finger at Elly. He then moved his hand as though he was writing in mid-air. Then again he pointed at Elly. He once again removed the glass vial from his chest pocket only to blatantly put it back, then yet again he pointed at Elly.

Elly thought, "What is he doing?" She held up her own hands as if to say, 'I don't understand.' Then a sound came to her, the sound matched the way the pilot was moving his mouth and the sound was, "Isshha," and again, "Issshhha." Then Elly saw a tear fall from the pilot's eyes and a huge wave of pity and sadness engulfed her.

In a flash, the scene changed, cold water now surrounded Elly. The young man was no longer there; the aircraft had vanished. Elly could feel her lungs fill with water, she began to choke, panic consumed her, she was underwater pulling with both arms, struggling against the downward pull, the pressure grew intense, she was being squeezed, there was no escape, and she screamed out in terror!

"Elly, Elly, wake up, wake up, you're dreaming. Elly wake up!" Tom was holding her by the shoulders, shouting into her face. Elly's arms were pulling at something; she was gulping for air, coughing, and spluttering.

Mol had jumped off the end of the bed and was standing still, her tail wagging nervously. She began to pant and her ears folded downwards, concern in her deep brown eyes.

"Come on Elly, wake up, you're dreaming!" Elly continued to fight with her invisible struggle; then she stopped suddenly. Her eyes opened wide, tears rolled down her cheeks, and she leapt off the bed heading for the door.

Mol quickly moved out of her way but followed at her heel. Tom looked on in complete surprise, 'Was she still in the dream?' He thought to himself.

Elly left the bedroom with a determined look on her face and said, in an excited tone, "I know what he means." Tom shouted after her, "Know what who means?" Elly ignored him and continued on her mission.

She opened the front door — it was still dark outside, but to the east, there was a hint of deep red in the sky.

She went to where she and Tom had taken off their diving

equipment and shouted over her shoulder, "I need a torch, Tom. Fetch a torch please." She began to rummage through the discarded equipment.

Tom arrived several seconds later.

Mol looked first at Elly then at Tom, a look of concern on her face. She took several steps toward Elly then back to Tom, the shock of seeing Elly fighting then flying out of the bed had spooked her, so she decided at that point to stick with Tom, and so she followed him closely just behind his legs. Sensing Mol's distress he bent down and patted her, "There, there everything is fine Mol," he said, gently. She looked up at Tom and almost said, 'But, what's going on then dad?'

Tom handed Elly the torch, "Thanks," she said.

"Elly, what the hell is going on, what are you doing?"

Elly replied, "I know what he wants Tom, can't you see?"

"Elly, I can't see anything, it's bloody dark. What do you mean, you know what he wants? Look, stop, tell me who he is and what he wants." Tom wanted to sound caring and sensitive, but Elly was scaring him. He had no idea what was happening and wondered if she was having a bad reaction to the diving incident. He stood and watched as Elly pulled at the pile of wet suits which she threw behind her. She said, "Yes, here it is!" She stood up straight and in her hands was her stab vest. She fumbled with the side pockets, shining the torch at the pocket and said, "He didn't want to pull me under, he was simply putting this into my pocket, he wanted me to look for it, Tom."

In the light of the torch Elly pulled a small item out of the side pocket of her stab jacket and she it held up. It was a small glass vial, in the top of which was a stopper with what appeared to be wax or glue around the rim. The glass was a dull grey colour but clearly looked as if it contained something.

Tom said, "Elly, stop, look at me. What on earth are you talking about, and who is he?"

Elly stood still as if stuck to the ground, saying, "Tom, the first night when I woke up, you remember? I saw his face, young, short, blond hair, and his eyes Tom, bright blue eyes. I know now it was him underwater, he was the one in the aircraft, he wanted me to have this." She held up the vial and continued, "Tom, don't you see he wants us to do something, let's open the vial and see what's inside."

The sky had started to change colour; a beautiful deep red-orange glow crept from the east over the distant landscape. A whole host of birds began to announce the dawn with their song. An early morning sea mist rolled across the seascape, gently moved by the lightest of sea breezes.

Elly and Tom went back into ' Driftwood'. Tom put the kettle on while Elly sat at the kitchen table looking at the vial. Mol was still outside, slightly confused with the emotions that her owners had just displayed. Then she entered the kitchen and sat down next to Elly lifting her paw in the air, her tail wagging. She wanted that reassuring, loving pat from Elly who obliged instantly and Mol lay down next to her.

Two tin mugs of tea were placed onto the kitchen table, steam rising, and it seemed like an eternity before the vial was touched.

It was sitting in the centre of the table, Elly sat on one side while Tom sat on the other. Elly said, "Do you think we should open it?" Tom said, "Well, I don't see why not. If you're saying that it was given to you, then I suppose it is meant to be opened. It would be crazy not to after what has happened."

Elly said, "I suppose you're right. You do it, though!"

Tom said, "Elly, it was given to you. You must open it."

Elly said, "But what if it's nothing?"

"Well, we'll find out any second. Look! Just open it, it won't bite you!"

Picking up the small vial, Elly attempted to pull the stopper out with her fingers, but it wouldn't budge. Then she took a small kitchen knife and gently eased the stopper, nothing at first, then it seemed to just pop out. Elly almost dropped the glass but managed to recover it and looked inside. Elly saw paper. She gingerly took hold of it with her nails and slowly pulled it out. All the time she had not taken a breath of air. Then with a deep breath, Elly unfolded the rolled-up paper. It had writing on it in very small text, which had been written with black pencil. With trembling hands, Elly looked at the tiny writing and started to read the words.

Iseabail Dearest.

Elly said, in an excited tone, "That's it, the word he was saying, Issshhh, it's Isobel, he was saying Isobel." Elly continued to read the note...

The timing of this wretched war has sent horror through my very heart. My abrupt departure from you and your most beautiful home has hurt most grievously, and I have so missed you over these long months.

My training with the German Luftwaffe is now at an end and yet I have hidden my most treasured intentions away from them. As I promised you, it is my intent to take an aircraft and fly to you as soon as an opportunity presents itself.

In composing this letter to you, it is my heart felt hope that you should never read it, but that I will express my wishes for us with you in person.

Papa died suddenly, and so I have no one left here. My home is in 'Driftwood' with you as it has always been destined. Until the time when we will spend the rest of our lives together, wait patiently my dearest.

Finally, as your name is derived and as I love God, so it is the same for you, my dear Iseabail.

Always Adler.

There was a reflective silence for several moments as, quietly weeping, Elly let the note drop from her hand. Tom picked it up and re-read it aloud, then fell silent.

Finally, he said, sombrely, "Elly, the note refers to here, to 'Driftwood,' Isobel must have lived here!"

They looked at each other and Elly said, "Oh Tom, he never made it. He was so close to his love, so close, what do we do now?"

Mol sensing the distress in the room, placed her head on Elly's lap, looking up as Elly looked down at her. Mol's tail wagged, and she licked Elly's hand. Elly smiled and said, through a tearful voice,

"Thank you, Mol, you are a dear friend."

Elly picked up the note and carefully returned it to the vial, replaced the stopper and put the vial on the table.

Outside the sun was rising fast, no longer an orange sky but the blue sky that promised another beautiful day next to the sea. Lightening the mood, Tom said, "Bacon and egg butties?" He stood up and opened the fridge for taking out a pack of bacon. Elly replied in a cheery tone, "Yes, why not, then perhaps a visit to the local library and see if we can find any information on Isobel and 'Driftwood.' It's so strange Tom, but I feel as though we were meant to come here, to stay in 'Driftwood'. Like I said, I feel comfortable here. Oh! I hope we can get some information." Elly began to weep, not out of sadness but some sort of happiness that the note had been located. Tom went and hugged her and, of course, Mol pushed in and nuzzled them both.

The kettle boiled — the whistle could be heard for miles it seemed — and the smell of bacon cooking made both of them feel hungry. Mol sat next to the cooker waiting with eager anticipation, drooling, her eyes making just enough contact to make a point. Tom looked at the clock, it was eight thirty. Bacon and egg butties were placed on the table, two fresh tin mugs full of hot tea were ready, and Mol was happily eating her breakfast, topped with a piece of bacon and chopped up fresh, local hen's egg! Spoiled or what!

Finishing their breakfast, Elly began to wash up the plates. There was a heavy knock at the door which made Elly jump. She looked at Tom who put his hands up with a questioning look. Mol attempted to bark but her mouth was full of egg and dog biscuits, and so the bark became a muffled coughing sound. There was another knock; Tom called out, "Yes, just coming."

He went to the front door and opened it. Standing on the doorstep was an elderly man with a tanned, weathered face, bright blue eyes and wearing an old, but beautifully laundered, tweed jacket, trousers, and polished mustard-coloured shoes. As the door opened, he took off his cap and dipped his head then said, in a soft Scottish accent, "I am sorry to be disturbing you on this beautiful morning, but I must talk with you." There was an edge to his opening statement.

Tom said, "Yes, please, come in. We're just having a cup of tea, would you like one?"

"Oh, t'would be too much trouble, I'm sure."

Tom said, "No, not at all, milk, sugar?" The stranger replied, "Little milk and two sugar, let it draw though!" Tom stirred the fresh pot of tea and let it stand for a couple of minutes.

During this time the stranger introduced himself as Angus McKinnon, a local fisherman who had lived on Great Cumbrae for all of his life.

Tom said, "Did we see you in the Inn?"

Angus replied, "Yes, you did, and I am so sorry for that old fool, he should have never said it, never!"

Elly said, "And how can we help?"

Angus said, slowly, "It is a long story. I don't know where I should begin!"

Elly said, "Well we are good listeners, so why not start at the beginning."

"Yes, good advice," said Angus.

Tom and Elly sat either side of the kitchen table, Angus sat at the end of the table, fidgeting his fingers. He seemed to be slightly on edge and would not make eye contact with them. He simply looked down at the cap in his hands. He cleared his throat and began to talk in a voice with a musical tone — Elly and Tom found him so easy to listen to.

"As you will know, gossip travels fast, well let me tell you, gossip travels even faster when you live on a small island! I knew I had to come and speak to you when I heard about your diving incident. Oh yes! Morag, the receptionist, has very big ears indeed and she heard most of your conversation with the good Doctor. What made me stop in my tracks was the description of what happened under the water, I mean to say 'the bubbles'.

"You see, I have held a secret for many long years, and over those long years, I have heard of many strange encounters just where you were diving.

"When I was a wee boy, I would play on the sea shore. Life was so much more simple then, entertaining yourself was easy, beach combing, watching how the tide ebbed and flowed, fishing, crabbing and gathering shellfish. Oh yes, gathering scallops was a real treat, they were in abundance, sadly not now, the damn Spanish came in and dragged the seabed and spoiled everything! But I go ahead of myself.

"I was about nine years old I suppose, playing right in front of this very cottage, 'Driftwood.' It was here that I got to know the owner of the cottage, Miss Matherson. She was beautiful, long dark hair, deepest brown eyes, and her smile, oh her smile! Miss Matherson had inherited the cottage from her great aunt, and you can imagine the gossip when a beautiful young girl moved onto the Isle, all by herself. It was a scandal particularly when she would go swimming in the sea, sometimes with very little clothing!" Angus flushed at this point, then continued, "She would gather scallops; it was gathering the scallops is how we met, oh we had such fun. The days were warm and long; I would come down here almost every day, but not on the Sabbath, no never, not unless you wanted to feel the wrath of the Minster! But I knew that Miss Matherson still had fun on the Sabbath.

Of course, it was wrong but, Oh! how I wish I could have such fun on the Sabbath, it just didn't seem fair.

"Time passed so slowly; I never wanted this time ever to finish. Miss Matherson would tell me stories about her travels — do you know she went to London and Paris? She told me about the huge Eiffel Tower and how you could see all of Paris. She also told me how she had travelled to the Americas on a ship that was almost bigger than this Island! Well you could imagine how exciting it was to hear such things and then she said to me, 'And one day my dear Angus, you will travel to see these wonderful places too.' The fact is that I have never really left the Isle, scratching a living from fishing is all I know." In silence, Angus looked at his hands for several moments then said, "It was about twelve months before the start of the terrible war with Germany. A visitor arrived on the Island, a German businessman and he brought with him his son, of course, they stayed in the Big House. They say that he, the father that is, paid well. And so they were welcome, I don't know what business he did, but it was something to do with boat building.

"One day while I was playing on the shore, I saw the young blond-haired, young man, tall and strong looking he was, with Miss Matherson. I remember feeling angry at seeing them together, you see I liked Miss Matherson but would never say so."

Angus went quiet for a while; his eyes welled with tears. But he gathered himself and continued, "So, where was I? Yes, it was clear that Miss Matherson and this German man got on very well. I know that it is not a good thing, but I was jealous I suppose, and so I hated that man, that he had taken Miss Matherson away from me. Oh, they would invite me into here for a home-made lemonade — I had never tasted it before, and I loved it. So it wasn't long before I started to like the German."

Elly butted in to ask, "This German, what was his name, can you remember?"

Angus replied, "Oh yes, how stupid of me, his name was Adler,

I never knew his second name, but it was Adler, and he told me that this meant 'eagle'. Well, I was even more impressed, Miss Matherson's friend was an eagle!

"Even at my age and even in my naivety I realised that they were in love. You could tell just by seeing how they looked at each other and how gentle and caring he was with her."

Elly said, "Was Miss Matherson's name Isobel?"

Angus looked up immediately and said, "Ee-she-bail, why yes, how on earth could you have known that?"

Elly did not respond.

Angus continued, "As the summer months went by, I saw less and less of Miss Matherson, I mean Iseabail. Of course, Adler was there most of the time, the women folk did not like this at all. Firstly Iseabail did not attend any services on the Sabbath, but more to the point, she was having a relationship with a German. I suppose the news about how Germany was acting and the threat of war made people intolerant.

"I remember on one occasion I saw Iseabail go into the store. I followed, just to be close to her. There were three locals in the shop, and when Iseabail entered, the others said, nasty things to her. I was proud of her though she took no notice of the women, she even smiled at them as she left the store. What was said, after she'd left, I find hard to repeat.

"It would seem that as the time went by, Adler's father decided that matters between Germany and Britain were so difficult that he had to return to his homeland, and that Adler was to go also.

"I crept up to 'Driftwood' and candles were burning in the windows. I could hear voices from inside. Iseabail was pleading with Adler to stay with her. She was crying so hard that I wanted to go straight in and comfort her, but I knew it was wrong. Unable to listen to any more I ran home.

"It was many weeks before I returned to visit Iseabail. Adler had left with his father, and within weeks war was declared.

It was a Sabbath, but I had to see Iseabail. So, quietly I sneaked out of the back of the Kirk and ran as fast as I could. When I arrived at 'Driftwood' I found the door open, so I knocked and went in. The kitchen was empty, then I heard weeping from the bedroom, and so I tapped on the door. 'Go away, I don't want to see anyone!' I whispered, 'But it's me, Angus, I've called to see if you are ok.' The door opened, and Iseabail stood in front of me, her face was changed, she was unkempt, her eyes were red, and her cheeks were wet with tears.

"I was angry to see her in such a state, and I showed it. I told her that I would make a mug of tea and that she was to join me in the kitchen. By the way, these here are the very same mugs.

"We sat down, and I told her that I was not happy to see her this way. She was very kind to me then and told me how sorry she was not to have taken much note of me when Adler was with her, 'He did like you, you know' she assured me. I felt guilty for thinking of him so badly.

"Then Iseabail told me of their plans and how Adler would leave Germany as soon as he could. She also said, that his father wanted him to join the German Luftwaffe, he wanted him to fly as this seemed a better wartime occupation. He did not want Adler fighting hand-to-hand on the front line. He felt that flying was safer. How wrong was he! Adler had promised Iseabail that as soon as he completed his training, he would steal an aircraft and fly back here."

Tom burst in, "He said, what, Angus, are you sure?"

"As sure as I have ever been, Sir," Angus replied.

Elly looked at Tom and, out of sight of Angus, she mouthed, "What?"

Continuing his story Angus said, "This was the last time I was to visit Iseabail because as we were talking, the door to the cottage crashed in and my father along with the Minster marched in. They told Iseabail that she was a wicked woman and that she was never to see me or my family again. The Minster told her that she was to burn in the fires of hell. They both left dragging me with them. I was never trusted by my father from that point, I was held on a tight leash."

Tears ran down the old man's face. He took an old but well-laundered handkerchief from his side pocket and softly blew his nose, apologising for his emotional outburst.

Elly went to his side and put her arms about him. Angus flinched then he allowed Elly to comfort him.

She said, "Angus, you have told us so much but what has any of this to do with us?"

Angus looked at both of them and said, "My tale has not yet finished; there is more to tell. You see, as the time went by, I kept a daily watch for any aircraft that might fly near our Island. The War had begun in earnest, but not much news reached us here. I continued to fish, that had become my full-time job. Feeding the community was vital as supplies were more difficult to get. Certain matters continued, the Sabbath for example, but not for me. I was no longer welcomed by the Minster. He felt that I had been corrupted and that God's work for me was to fish, to fish in all weathers and conditions. I was also compelled to take the catch to the Minster's home first, so that he could take the prime of the catch, the rest was shared between the families. It was on a Sabbath, I was fishing, and I'd rowed quite a way out to the south of the Island, the clouds were low, and it was windy. That is when I saw it, the plane. It came over quite low, and I only saw it briefly, and then it vanished, but what I did see was a black cross on the tail. I knew it must be Adler; he had kept his promise. Iseabail would be happy again. I rowed as hard as I could back to shore. I ran towards 'Driftwood' — I do not know what I was expecting to see, but there was nothing, nothing at all.

"I could not believe that there was no evidence of a plane or a landing, or smoke but there was nothing.

"I have never told a living being this tale until now as I believe that you have seen something under the water that might just confirm what I have said, You see, I believe that I have seen him!"

There was an uncomfortable silence in the small kitchen, Angus looked at Tom and then at Elly.

Elly said, "What ever became of Iseabail?"

Angus replied, "She was never accepted into the community following these events, and I never saw her again for many, many years. When I did see her again, she was not the same beautiful woman that I had loved — you see I never married — the woman I loved was taken from me."

Elly interrupted, "So are you saying that Iseabail has passed away?"

Angus replied, "No! She is still with us. She lives in the nursing home at the top of the Island. She has been there for many years, but she has not spoken a single word to any one since taking up residence there at the end of the War. I have visited her in recent years, but she just sits and looks out of the windows. It would seem that she paid for a private room at the home, and that her staff are not locals. It is said, that Iseabail is a very wealthy lady. Why she still owns this cottage, but only lets it out once or twice a year, you are the first this year. She was such a wonderful lady, but since that time I would say that she has never given up waiting for Adler to return."

Elly and Tom exchanged glances once more. Mol stretched on the floor and went back to sleep.

Elly said, "Angus, I did see something under the water. I also saw someone standing in the bedroom."

Angus said, "That is where I saw him. I caretake 'Driftwood,' and one day I saw Adler, oh, he didn't frighten me at all, I was just happy that he was here. You are the first and last I will tell this story to. I am old but needed to tell someone who would understand. I'm content now, and it would seem that it is up to you two now!"

With a nod of his head, Angus stood up, thanked them for his tea, touched his cap and left.

Looking shaken Elly said to Tom, "We have to see Miss

Matherson. She must be given this vial and the letter. Poor, poor woman, she has waited so long and for what? She was never given a chance by the locals; it must have been terrible, just terrible for her. We must contact the home and see her now!"

Tom said, "Elly, let's think about this. We cannot just barge in on her and say, 'oh by the way here's what you have been waiting for,' hand her the note and leave!"

Elly replied, "Tom, I know this might sound odd, but I believe that is what we are supposed to do. I just sense that it's right. Please trust me on this one."

Tom replied, "Ok, it's your call, let's go and get it over with."

'Great Cumbrae House' is an imposing three-storey Victorian house, now being used as a nursing care home. The house was converted during World War Two into a nursing home where injured soldiers would spend recovery time. After the War, it was continued to be run as a care home.

In time Elly and Tom would find out that the home was not only Miss Matherson's but, in fact, she had privately and unknown to locals donated vast amounts of funds to keep it running. Ironically the home cared for quite a few of those people who did not like Miss Matherson!

Elly and Tom were taken to a waiting room where they were offered refreshments. After about ten minutes the door opened, and a sturdy looking nurse pushed a wheel chair into the room. Almost lost in the chair sat a tiny woman, her hair mostly silver white and her skin white but with slight rosy hints on her cheeks. Her eyes were the deepest chestnut brown, and they sparkled. Miss Iseabail Matherson was pushed to the side of a pair of window seats where the view was over the west coast of Great Cumbrae and also to the shore line where 'Driftwood' stood.

The nurse spoke in a soft Welsh tone, "These are the youngsters who have come to visit. This is Elly and Tom."

With this introduction complete the nurse left the room.

There was a strange silence as Iseabail seemed to be studying the pair now seated in the window seats. Then in a frail but clear voice, she said, "I've been waiting for you for such a long time, but I knew that you would come."

Elly said, "Miss Matherson, we were informed that you did not speak?" Iseabail said, "It has made life for me easier to bear, not to talk about," her voice became shaky, but she regained control and went on, "to talk about Adler. Yes, I see that you are aware. I suspect that dear little Angus has spoken with you. Oh! I have not treated that sweet wee boy so well. He was in love with me did he tell you?"

Tom replied, "Yes he did, he was very fond of you and so saddened that he was forbidden to see you."

She replied, "It was for the best as I had only one love in my life and that, as you know, was Adler. I waited for him to return and then, as the time went by, I realised that he had probably been lost in the War, but something kept me going. It was a belief, a belief that he would one day be with me. I have felt him close. It would have been so wrong of me to have spoken about him to anyone and so I kept my silence. After a time it is easy. People think that you are quite mad if you cannot or will not speak and they treat you differently. That is why I chose to live here instead of at 'Driftwood'.

It is quite amazing what you can glean when you concentrate and learn to listen carefully. That is how I knew that you would come here. I listened to people talking, and so now you are here, and you have something to tell me?"

Elly said, "But how did you know we would come to see you?"

She replied, "There are many things you can do if you try. As I said, I listened carefully, that's all."

Elly stood up and took the small glass vial from her jacket pocket and held it out to Iseabail.

Elly said, "We believe that this belongs to you. I have to be honest, I have read the contents, and that is how we know it is yours. Would you like me to open it?" Iseabail nodded.

Once again, Elly removed the stopper and retrieved the note from within. She said, "Would you like me to read it to you?" The reply surprised both Elly and Tom. "No, even though most functions are old and rusted my eyes are perfect. I have trained them on the shore for too many years to remember, so — no — I can read as well as ever, thank you, Elly." Handing Iseabail the hand-written note, Elly felt a huge pang of sadness.

Lifting the note up to her eyes Iseabail read and, when she had finished, she placed it on her lap. Tiny tears ran down her pale, silk-like cheeks. She looked out of the window and said, "Thank you, my dear Elly. You have brought me what I needed. I am happy now knowing that Adler kept his promise and that he was indeed near to me as I always felt, thank you."

There was a brief pause, then she said, "Now tell me, what do you think of 'Driftwood'?"

Elly replied, "Well, I feel so at home there, so comfortable and happy, yes it is a happy home."

Iseabail said, "Yes it is, I loved that dear small cottage. You are correct it is a happy home, perhaps one day I might return to it."

Iseabail pressed a small button on her chair, the door opened, and the nurse walked in. To her absolute surprise, Iseabail said, to her, "My dear, you can now show these wonderful people out. It was an absolute pleasure." Iseabail continued to look out of the window.

The nurse, still in shock at hearing Iseabail talking for the very first time, showed Elly and Tom to the main door where they said, their goodbyes.

Returning to 'Driftwood' Elly and Tom felt drained of all emotion and energy. Mol greeted them enthusiastically running in and out of the kitchen being in a very good and playful mood. She wasn't able to tell her owners about the fun she'd enjoyed with the special visitor while they were out!

The next couple of days went without incident. Tom and Elly walked with Mol and beach-combed. Mol, of course, loved being the centre of attention pushing herself in between Elly and Tom, just in case they forgot that she was there! They were completely at ease in the little croft cottage on the sea shore. Then while walking bare-footed along the shore, Elly stopped and looked longingly out to sea. Mol sat next to her and looked up at her face, her loving eyes seemed to want to ask a question, but it was Mol's nose that was indicating something in the air. Her nostrils sucked in the sea breeze then she sneezed and shook her head, she repeated this several times. Elly turned to Tom and said, in a casual tone, "Shall we go and look for the aircraft again? I just have to know if Adler's remains are still down there, and if so, we can mark the spot with a view to recovering his remains in the future."

Tom agreed, so they started to put their diving equipment together. Mol trotted along the shore with her head held high; she was inhaling then shaking her head. She ran back to Elly and Tom and within what seemed only a minute or so a sea breeze picked up and started to blow. White topped waves began to crash over the rocks and then up onto the shoreline, sea spray covered the three of them, Mol sneezed and shook her head once more. There was nothing in the forecast that had predicted this weather front. Diving conditions deteriorated almost instantly. Diving was off.

Removing their equipment, Tom said, "Look. Clearly, we won't be diving now, so why not pack up and just sit this weather out. I'll do dinner and light a fire." Mol seemed to smile at this comment and trotted happily home.

Disappointed, Elly had to agree.

The weather continued to deteriorate, the wind howled, and the waves increased in size crashing over the shore. The birds who were also taken by surprise huddled in tall grasses. Sea foam flew across the pebbles and stuck momentarily to the cottage windows. The best place to be was safely indoors.

Elly opened a bottle of wine and sat in front of the fire watching the flames licking the air and escaping up the chimney. Molly cuddled into her side and looked nervously at the door as another gust of wind hit the gable. Elly stroked Mol's head and spoke softly to her which reassured her. She stretched out and began to twitch as she fell asleep.

The local station which they got on the small DAB radio, expressed concern over the sudden and wild weather conditions, which were not forecast for another two days. Strangely, Elly was quite happy to sit out the storm in here; as she had said to Miss Matherson, she felt at home and happy in the cottage.

Dinner was served — fresh, seared scallops and steaming hot buttered, new potatoes — eaten by candle light. After dinner, they simply continued to listen to the storm and the crashing of the waves just outside, but the fire kept them warm and cosy. On the sheepskin rug in front of the fire, Elly, Tom, and Mol enjoyed each other's company and felt quite safe. They eventually went to their bed. Of course, Mol took the space in between Elly and Tom and stayed there all night like a hot water bottle for the sleeping pair.

They were due to leave the Island the following day as they had to return to work on the Monday. Elly asked Tom, while he was packing, "Would you mind if I visit Miss Matherson? I would like to say goodbye to her." Tom said, "No, that's a great idea and take Mol with you, so I don't have her around my feet while I'm packing."

Elly drove the short distance to the nursing home, Mol taking her position as a front seat passenger. This was her car after all and when Tom was not in the car the front seat was hers! Arriving at the home, Elly rang the bell and waited several minutes before the same nurse as before opened the door. It was clear that she'd been crying and just indicated for Elly to come in. Then she was able to say, "Oh! I thought you were the locum; you see Miss Matherson passed away during the night. It was quite a peaceful passing, in fact. I don't know what you said, to her, but she was so animated and talkative when you left. She seemed so very happy."

Elly said, "May I see her? I don't know why but I would just like to say goodbye to her."

"Absolutely, and by the way, she must have known that you would come back because she left this for you."

The nurse pulled a small envelope out of her pocket. Elly felt it and realised that it was the vial, so she popped it into her jacket pocket and followed the nurse.

Climbing the stairs, Elly felt sadness at hearing the news, but she also felt a sort of relief for Iseabail. It would seem that her waiting was indeed over and she could at last rest in peace. The nurse opened the door on a huge bedroom, beautifully decorated with soft furnishings, books, and paintings. Elly went to the bed and looked on Iseabail and felt as if she was in the most comfortable peaceful sleep. She even appeared to have a smile on her lips. Elly leaned over her and kissed her on the forehead and said, "Rest well my dear Iseabail, find Adler and be at last together."

Elly crossed the room to the large bay window. She could clearly see 'Driftwood' on the shore. Closing her eyes Elly summoned the vision of Adler and Iseabail, she saw them approach each other. A tear of happiness fell from her eyes. Elly wondered about the events that had unfolded and how odd but beautiful the outcome could be, star crossed lovers reunited, it was a true love story, and she was part of it. This brought a smile to her face, she turned away from the window and walked across the room where she thanked the nurse and left. Elly got back into her car and sat for a few seconds still reflecting. Mol looked across to Elly, her eyes soft and understanding, the tip of her tail wagging; she reached across and licked Elly's face which made her smile and Elly ruffled Mol's head.

When Elly got back to the cottage, Tom had all but completed the packing. She told Tom about Miss Matherson, and what the nurse had said, Tom said, "It looks like she was just waiting to hear from Adler and now she can rest in peace."

"The strange thing, Tom, is that she expected me to return to the home because she gave this to the nurse to give to us!" Elly then produced the vial. Tom said, "Come on Elly, how on earth could she know that you would go back?" A little hurt by the comment Elly replied, "Well there have been also lots of strange events, and this is just one of them!"

Feeling bad about his comment, Tom said, in a caring tone, "Ok Elly, perhaps we should leave the vial somewhere in here — this is where it now belongs, don't you think?" Elly said, "Yes, but don't you think we should hide it? I mean it is part of this building's beautiful story, so it needs to be literally inside. What do you think?" Tom gave Elly an old-fashioned look but agreed.

They looked around the cottage for a hiding place, then Elly called to Tom, "Look, I think I've found the perfect spot!"

Just to the side of the hearth was a small loose stone. Elly went to move it, and it just fell out. Behind where the stone had been was a space which was the right size for the vial.

"What do you think?" Elly asked. Tom looked at the space and said, "Well, it could have been made for that vial, see if it fits."

Elly offered the vial up to the hole, and it fitted in perfectly, then she replaced the stone. It looked like nothing had been tampered with.

Tom called the ferry company and was advised to take the next departure as the weather front was deepening and it was more than likely that all ferry services would be suspended. They were away within the hour.

Several months passed and Elly and Tom settled back into their usual lives. Molly took up her usual dog routine, walk first thing, then house guard followed by fun and more walking later in the day. Saturday's were the best as they all went for a long walk.

One sunny Saturday morning, Elly and Tom had, unusually, slept in. Mol had no such thoughts, and she'd tried to get their attention, first by jumping onto the bed, then by face licking — that always did the trick. The three of them were playing games on the bed when the doorbell rang. Mol went into action. Flying off the bed and down the stairs, she jumped at the door and gave a friendly but 'watch out big dog here!' bark.

Elly pulled on her dressing gown and followed her down to open the front door. Standing on the doorstep was a delivery man.

"Two for you today Elly, they need to be signed for. Good morning Molly." Mol stood and wagged her tail at the familiar deliveryman. Elly said, "Very kind, thank you, Dave. Usual place?" Elly signed and took the two parcels then closed the door. It was when the door was closed that Elly saw a letter on the mat beneath the post box. Picking it up she saw that the post mark was from Paris.

Elly went to the kitchen where she placed the items on the kitchen table; then she made a pot of tea. She sat down and opened the letter with the intriguing postmark first. She was not expecting anything from Paris neither did she know anyone who lived there. Inside the envelope was a photograph, which she put to one side, and began to read the letter.

Dear Elly and Tom,

I felt that I must send you this letter, firstly to thank you for listening to me all those months ago and secondly to inform you of the following.

As you are aware, my Iseabail passed away, and I was the only one at her funeral which took place in the 'Shore Burial Ground' that overlooks the sea.

I have to tell you that Iseabail left me a note in which she expressed her 'special love' for me and told me to take her advice and see the sights she had told me about. She had enclosed a passport form and enough money to go where and when I liked. As you can see from the photograph, I am in Paris, and I have seen London and will be travelling on the new Queen Elizabeth, going to America.

Elly picked up the enclosed photograph and standing in front of the Eiffel Tower was Angus wearing a very smart tweed jacket and breeks, and shining brown shoes. He was holding his hat in his hands; his head slightly bowed as though he was nodding at Elly. He had a huge, warm smile on his face.

Elly called for Tom to come down straight away, tears of joy and laughter rolling down her face. When Tom entered, he asked, "What's up?" Elly pointed at the photograph and said, "It's dear Angus, he looks so happy."

Returning to the letter Elly read on.

I can only tell you the next bit of information. Just after you left the Island the front turned into a deeper, intense storm, the ferry was cancelled, all power was lost, and many properties were damaged. Thankfully, there were no casualties. The Island was a mess. However, a local fisherman who was out searching for his small boat, found more than he bargained for. On the shoreline in front of 'Driftwood' he found the remains of a body. There were no identifying features. In fact, it was almost a skeleton. As soon as this news spread, I knew immediately who it was — Adler. At last, he'd found home. The other strange thing is, no aircraft parts or debris were found, it seems that it just disappeared.

And so, as there was no way to identify the remains, no missing persons' reports, and even after looking into very old files, there was nothing for the Police to go on. After several months, the

Coroner ruled that because of lack of evidence, the remains should be buried.

Elly, Tom! Adler was buried next to Iseabail, right next to her. We must keep what we know between ourselves.

I hope to see you in the future.

Your good friend

Angus.

Tom and Elly sat in silence for several moments, then Elly said, "Oh Tom, now they're together, after all this time. Together! It is beautiful."

Tom agreed and said, "What's in the other envelope?"

Picking it up Elly carefully opened the large white, official-looking envelope and inside were official-looking documents. She read the opening letter...

'Dear Mr. and Mrs. James.

Please find attached a copy of the Last Will and Testament of the late, Iseabail Matherson. I have been instructed to pass to Mr. Thomas and Mrs. Elly James, the Title Deeds to 'Driftwood', West Coast, Great Cumbrae.

You will also have been in receipt of a box. Please open the box and inside you will find the keys to the said, property. I have informed the local land registry office.

To see the full details of the Will, or if you have any question, please do not hesitate to call.

Yours sincerely.

Bruce Donaldson.

Elly looked open-mouthed at Tom. Tom took hold of the box and carefully opened it.

Inside were two tin mugs, inside one mug was a set of keys, in the other a handwritten note. Tom took the note and read it out.

My Dearest Elly and Tom
With great happiness, I now give you 'Driftwood'. It is my last wish that you have as much happiness and fun as I ever did. Thank you. Iseabail.

Arriving on Great Cumbrae Elly and Tom drove straight to the burial ground. They quickly located the headstone belonging to Iseabail and placed a bunch of fresh flowers in front of it. Bowing their heads, they said, 'thank you' to her and then looked at the next grave. There was no headstone, but there was a large granite stone about the size and shape of a rugby ball and etched into the stone was a golden eagle in flight. Tom and Elly then bowed their heads in respect to Adler. Elly said, "And at last you are next to your beloved, be well with each other for the rest of time." They said, their goodbyes and left for their new home.

Elly and Tom opened the door to 'Driftwood' and Mol picked up where she had left off the last time, running along the shore chasing the oystercatchers, her head held high, her nostrils inhaling the sea air and of course, Mol's tail was like a propeller. Once over the threshold Elly and Tom stood in silence for several seconds as they both took in the fact that this cottage, 'Driftwood', now belonged to them. Opening a bottle of bubbly, Tom poured it into the tin mugs, and they stood in the doorway looking out to sea, raised the mugs and Tom said, "To Iseabail and Adler, thank you."

It had been a long and emotional day, Elly and Tom thought at some length about the events that had led to this moment. Molly lay in front of the glowing fire, exhausted following the chase, but she was happy, and she could sense the feeling of happiness both in the cottage and between her best friends.

Shortly after dinner, scallops and new buttered potatoes, they went to bed. Mol, of course, took her usual place on the bed and immediately went to sleep where she twitched and almost 'blew raspberries' when she exhaled.

While Elly slept, she became aware that her face was being softly brushed and she woke up to find Mol wagging her tail across both their faces. Tom stirred and woke up. Elly nudged him and whispered, "Tom, look in the corner!" Lifting his head from the pillow, Tom looked into the corner of the room. It appeared to be filled with tiny, faint fireflies flitting around, then coming into focus, two ghostly figures appeared, a beautiful young woman with long brown hair and deep hazel eyes. She was smiling at Elly and Tom. Standing next to her was a tall, blond-haired young man. He too was smiling at them. The figures were holding hands, then Iseabail mouthed 'Thank you', and blew them a kiss. Adler bowed his head, and they both faded away. A warmth entered the room together with a light which faded as Iseabail and Adler vanished.

With tears in their eyes, Elly turned to Tom and kissed him full on his lips then she said, through a happily weeping voice, "Beautiful, it is so beautiful!" Mol took her place in between them and licked their faces.

CREEK FALLS

They say the drop over Creek Waterfall is more than two-hundred feet. As Tom held firmly onto the handrail and looked over the edge he heard or rather, felt a scream, a blood curdling echo of terror, which made his stomach turn, and his body became heavy; all he wanted to do was close his eyes and run.

It had been a difficult decision for Tom and Elly to holiday anywhere else than their beloved cottage on the shore on the Isle of Cumbrae. They had inherited 'Driftwood' from its elderly owner following a very special time there. Elly, in particular, adored the sense of love and peace they'd found, although her initial experiences had been quite frightening. It was a special place, too, for Molly, their springer spaniel, who loved to go twice a year to count the rabbits and run along the sands. But after Molly had the puppies, she'd taken a while to get fit again and had lost some of her old agility. Trying to negotiate a stile on one of their local walks she'd caught a back leg and dislocated a joint, tearing the tendons into the bargain. With their annual holidays already booked, Tom and Elly decided they couldn't face being at 'Driftwood' without her. They had kept one of her puppies, a strong, affable male they'd named, 'Cosmo' and as he approached a year-old it seemed like a perfect time to take him on his first camping trip. Out of the blue, Tom's sister, Helen, had offered to look after Molly as she wasn't needing her usual long walks. Elly worried that they'd come home and find their formerly fit springing springer had turned into a sofa-bound barrel, but Tom shrugged and said they'd only be away for a week; what harm could be done in that time? The dog was under strict orders from the vet that she rest. It would be perfect and much easier for Helen to say 'no' to those begging eyes and wagging tail. So they grabbed their chance, packed the tent and camping gear together with Cosmo and headed north.

In the old VW estate car, that was still going strong, Cosmo took a couple of minutes looking forlornly out of the rear window wondering why he was being separated from his mother for the first time. He whined just a little until Elly reassured him that he would love camping. As they drove onto the motorway, he did half a dozen circles on his blanket, tucked his nose under his paw and went to sleep.

Elly knew about the Tall Trees campsite from her childhood days holidaying in an ancient towed caravan of which her father had been ridiculously proud. She'd seen most of Scotland on those tours and never really felt she wanted to go anywhere else. When Helen had given them the chance to get away, she and Tom had spent an evening with the maps laid out on the kitchen table, throwing suggestions at each other; checking who took dogs and where it was possible to walk straight out from the site and into the hills. Elly had phoned her Mum; she could remember, as a small girl, walking up the side of a very big waterfall — where had that been? Mum had known straightaway and rambled off on a reminiscence that lasted over an hour. There had been tears as she remembered the silly things Elly's father had done to keep them entertained and that set Elly off too, still sensitive over four years' since they'd lost him. As she soothed her mother's tears, she grabbed the right map with her free hand and pointed out the site, close to Glen Affric, to Tom. He looked a little dubious at first. By the time Elly put the phone down, he'd calculated the length of the long drive into the Highlands.

"Early start," was Elly's response, "two hours each and a good stretch for Cosmo at each change. If we're camping, it doesn't matter what time we arrive. Please, Tom. I'd love to go back there, and you'll love it too, and so would Cosmo, wouldn't you boy?" She looked across at a keen face and bright eyes watching them closely from his basket by the Aga while Molly slept soundly beside him.

"He'll go wild! He won't know which smell to follow first. But we mustn't tell Molly yet; she'll be so disappointed."

Tom pretended he still wasn't sure whether they should go so far and whether Helen would cope if Mol pined for them, but really he was teasing Elly, and he couldn't hold out for very long. Eventually, he turned on a broad grin and gave her the thumbs up.

***

The campsite was surrounded by mature Scots Pine trees, tall and open canopied so unlike the plantation conifers that blanket great parts of the land. Under the pines, heather and bilberry thrive; there are red squirrels and pine martens if you're lucky. In summer there's a buzz of insect life, and butterflies and dragonflies patrol the glades. When it's hot, the scent of the pines is magical. There are many easy paths weaving through the trees following streams up into the Glen where patches of the ancient Caledonian pine forest stalk across more open hillsides. Elly remembered seeing deer here early one morning holding her father's hand, being implored to stay silent.

At the end of the long drive they'd pitched their old orange tent — Tom's contribution from his scouting days but, as he insisted, still very serviceable — and given Cosmo a quick run around the trails that spidered out from the site.

Elly and Tom were woken early by bright sunlight flooding into the tent and as soon as he sensed them stirring, by a cold, wet nose and much licking. Cosmo bounced between one sleeping bag and the other until Tom hauled himself into some clothes and, attaching a lead to Cosmo's collar, took him a jog through the forest while Elly roused herself more leisurely and got a camp breakfast underway.

Tom arrived back with one very wet spaniel looking very pleased with himself. He shook himself all over her legs which made her laugh and scream.

"He spotted a duck," Tom explained as he got his breath back. "There's an almost overgrown lochan up the way, and Cosmo didn't realise there was water. He just took off and fell right in. I'll say this; he's a stronger swimmer than Mol! We'll have to keep an eye on him though; we can't have him chasing the wildlife like that."

Elly bent to give Cosmo a rub under his chin, which signalled to him that he could rub his soaking wet coat up her legs. She danced out of his way and went to the car to fetch his towel and his breakfast bowl. Very soon, he was stretched out in the sunshine drying off and snoozing while Tom and Elly had their bacon buttie breakfast and planned their day.

The forecast was excellent, and they decided on a walk of about eight miles, winding up alongside of the river then climbing up to the famous waterfall. They'd read a little about it; how a small meandering stream flowed gently from the higher ground, picking up speed as the gradient increased and being forced between the walls of a narrow gorge in a series of rapids before finally launching itself over a spectacular drop into a dark, moody, damp place where there is little light. The photographs on the Web looked amazing, and Tom and Elly were quite surprised at how few people were on the trail. They guessed that the four-mile hike in must deter a lot of folk and the busy school holidays were also over. They told each other how lucky they were to have the place to themselves.

As soon as they felt it was safe, they let Cosmo off his lead and did some reinforcement training to keep him quartering around them, snuffling in and out of the undergrowth but never straying too far. Once he got the hang of it, he would keep returning to their heels, wagging his tail furiously and looking very pleased with his performance. Very soon his long ears were full of twigs and other adornments, but they didn't bother him.

"I'll take the comb to those ears, young pup!" Elly called after him, but Cosmo was already following the next trail of scents.

They strolled on in silence listening to the birds and a light breeze rustling the leaves of the silver birches that mix in with the pines higher up. Their leaves were already starting to turn yellow, and soon the Glen would turn on its autumn colour show ahead of winter's snows. Tom said, "We'll have to come again a little later in the year. Let's treat ourselves to a week at the Lodge or the Hotel, perhaps?"

"Let's see what the Hotel's like first. You did book it for tomorrow, didn't you? And told them about Cosmo?"

"Of course. We have the only spaniel who prefers luxury hotels to the excitement of camping. Didn't mention I had a wife though." He poked Elly in the ribs and dashed off laughing before she could get him back.

A little way further on Cosmo stopped suddenly in front of them. He was stiff and pointing forwards, his ears perked. Tom and Elly looked at each other and shrugged.

"What is it young pup?" Elly whispered then she heard the sound herself. A barking, barking, barking not very far off now. Cosmo turned to check that it would be OK for him to investigate. Elly sent him off. Soon there were combined barks, and Cosmo crashed out of the undergrowth twenty yards ahead of them followed very closely by the other dog. They raced around and round in circles playing tag until Cosmo eventually drew his new-found friend up to Tom and Elly to introduce him.

Tom bent to ruffle the dog's chest. He was about the same size as Cosmo but with a lion-like ruff and deep golden eyes that seemed to stare straight through Tom. It made him shiver, and he couldn't understand why; a dog had never had this effect on him before.

Elly bent beside him, "Hello, fella. You are beautiful, aren't you?" No sooner were these words said than Cosmo nuzzled under her arm and demanded her attention, "And you're the jealous one!" She stood up, and the dogs took off into a fresh session of 'catch me if you can'.

"Isn't that dog a little strange?" Tom said. "I wonder where his owner is."

"How do you mean, 'strange'?" Elly replied.

"Well, you're usually the sensitive one. You saw the ghost at 'Driftwood'. It's just that he kind of gave me the creeps when I touched him."

"Nope. Just a lovely dog who seems to have become detached from his owner. Cosmo seems to like him. Good job it's not a she or we'd be having to haul him off her!"

They walked on into a clearing beside the river accompanied by both dogs. By then they'd decided the other dog must be local as it seemed to know its way around and showed no signs of being lost. They guessed it would find its way home when it was ready.

They stopped for refreshment and sat down on a huge log. As they took a drink and ate some biscuits, Elly watched a flock of finches darting about in a nearby birch tree. She broke off a bit of biscuit, crumbled into her palm and outstretched her arm towards the birds offering the crumbs. A finch landed on her finger, then flitted away again, but seconds later it was back. This time it hopped up to her palm and collected a beak full before flitting back to the tree. Soon a regular stream of chaffinches was coming and going from Elly's hand and then Tom joined in. They were surrounded by twittering birds which, much to Cosmo's frustration, he could get nowhere near. The other dog sat a little away from the activity seeming to watch but not participate. Tom offered him a half a biscuit, but he simply looked down at his paws as though this were not something he could condone. The biscuit disappeared nonetheless as Cosmo taking a leap in from behind extracted it from Tom's hand in one deft movement.

"Hey! That wasn't for you, piglet." Tom shouted after him, but Cosmo wasn't listening. He'd run to sit beside his friend as he finished off the treat. The friend looked once at Cosmo, a cold stare down his snout, and returned his eyes to Tom; that piercing, hard look that seemed so different to Cosmo's darting glances, always looking for fun if not mischief.

They set off again, and the dogs settled into a calm trot next to them as they started to press uphill.

"I wonder if he has a name? There's no tag. What shall we call you?" Tom asked not expecting an answer. The dog woofed and woofed again. "Elly, he's trying to tell us his name." The dog barked, not a loud bark but a soft, responsive bark. "OK, I've got it. I know who you are. You're 'barker', no, that's not quite right. Say it again." The dog responded to Tom and barked once more. "You're 'Barkly!'" Tom exclaimed, and the dog bowed its head and looked across at Cosmo as if to say how slow his owners were to understand a simple name.

Climbing higher the air was fresh and cool, and they could hear the crashing water of the fall. A pair of golden eagles circled high above them as they reached the viewpoint.

***

"Tom? Are you alright?" Elly shouted and stopped jumping up and down on the end of the loose platform suspended above the fall. She'd persuaded him to walk the plank to try to exorcise his fear of heights and couldn't resist teasing him by making it wobble; she thought, just a little. While she laughed, Tom was terrified. The scream, he knew, must have been inside his mind,

GREAT STORIES WRITTEN BADLY

the image one of watching himself falling from the planks and slipping into the abyss below. What was worse was the sense that he was actively throwing himself there; this was no accidental slip, he was wishing it to happen. He dropped to his hands and knees and crawled back towards Elly who was, at last, starting to show some concern.

Tom looked up at his wife. "Satisfied? There I did it, now will you give it a rest!" He said, angrily.

As soon as he reached good solid ground his fears and the weird feeling of wanting to throw himself over the edge vanished. What strange games our minds play, he thought, as he stayed on his knees letting Elly's concern grow, just for a minute or two. Then he lightly touched her ankle, sprang up and chased her through the trees. By the time he caught her, they were both laughing. He swung her into his arms and kissed her firmly on the lips. They fell into the soft heather where Tom took his revenge by tickling Elly just at the base of her ribcage, sending her into fits of giggles. She tried to get to her feet, but he pulled her back down thinking how quiet and beautiful the spot was. He started to make love forgetting that somewhere in the woods happily amusing himself was their young springer spaniel, Cosmo. Cosmo, with supreme timing, now turned up and thought this was a great game of wrestling. He jumped on and off their bodies and barked himself into a frenzy, racing backwards and forwards, leaping and twisting in the air. What a gang of fools!

The moment passed; Tom rolled onto his back then sat up breathing heavily and laughing aloud. He called to Cosmo to calm, and the dog came and snuggled his snout under Tom's arm. "Such a good boy." Tom whispered to him.

"You look like you have a bird's nest on your head. I half expected a couple of fledglings to peek out with their mouths open squawking for food!" Tom picked at stalks tangled in Elly's long blond hair. He stroked a finger along her lower jaw and trailed it down her neck. Elly shook him away realising that it was really a very public place. Anyone could come along the footpath.

As Elly pulled herself up into a sitting position, pressing her palms on the ground, she suddenly yelped in pain, a flush of heat raced through her entire body, her eyes rolled, and she slumped backwards onto the heather.

"Elly! Elly, what's wrong?" Tom sank to his knees beside her and lifted her unconscious body into his arms. Cosmo, seemingly realising that his mistress wasn't well came and sat at her feet, his head cocked, waiting instructions.

Tom stroked the hair away from Elly's face. "Wake up, please Elly. Wake up!"

***

Elly found herself standing in front of a small lake, half of its surface covered with beautiful, pale purple lilies. The clear water reflected bright blue skies and a shimmering white house which stood on the opposite shore. Looking across to it she could make out grand double doors sitting centrally between an array of tall sash windows. A protruding upper portico was supported on four stucco columns and leading up to the entrance was a wide splay of stone steps. It was an impressive building. Elly felt drawn to it and was that someone moving across the top step?

***

"Elly, Elly wake up!" Her husband's voice filtered into her consciousness, and she opened her eyes only to close them tight against the bright sunlight.

"Where am I?" she whispered, disoriented.

"I think you must have fainted or something. Perhaps you got a bit overheated with us fooling around," Tom said in a gentle voice.

"No, no, I don't think so. My hand hurt; something stabbed my hand." She looked at her left hand and rubbed at a small red mark that hurt far more than it should have.

"Perhaps it was a sting, an ant or a snake, perhaps?" Tom suggested.

"No, I felt something hard under my hand...and don't you go frightening me with talk of snakes."

"It could have been. There are plenty in these woods, you know."

"Shut up! Let me look around."

She reached out and felt gingerly around in the undergrowth.

"It was just here; I know it was." With that, her fingers touched a small object that she thought at first might just be a sharp pebble, but as she picked it out of the soil and cleaned it off, she found it was much more interesting.

In Elly's hand lay a gold earring adorned with turquoise, blood red and black enamelling with small turquoise stones hanging along the rim.

"It looks Indian to me," Elly said holding it up for Tom to inspect. "I wonder if it's solid gold."

"Could be," Tom replied, "it's not tarnished at all. Bit of a strange place to find it so far off the path." He offered her his hand to pull her to her feet.

"Gently does it. How's the head? I nearly freaked when you passed out. Are you OK now?"

"Yes, I'm fine," Elly said, slightly subdued. "Come on, let's carry on and find somewhere for lunch." She wrapped the earring in a tissue and stowed it in the pocket of her fleece jacket.

"Are you sure we shouldn't just take the quickest descent and get you checked over?"

"Tom! Please don't fuss. It's not like my diving accident when I saw the...when I got caught in that eddy current. I just blanked for a moment; it's nothing. Where's Cosmo and do we still have Barkly attached?"

"He was here just a moment ago. Must have got bored the moment he could see you were OK."

Tom whistled, and their dog arrived at his heels in a few seconds, having kept a watchful eye on them from a little way off. Barkly was there but kept his distance until they were well away from the Falls. A little way further on they found a shelf of rock that gave them a great view from high in the upper glen all the way down to where the river ran away south-eastwards. They ate their lunch and drowsed in the sunshine while the dogs sniffed and snuffled in the surrounding heather. Fully rested, Tom took Elly's hand and pulled her to her feet. He kissed her forehead and led her back onto the path.

***

The dogs were now not so playful and appeared subdued as they both walked closely alongside the couple. They descended into a narrow tree-lined lane, peaceful in the dappled sunlight that penetrated the woodland and illuminated large mounds of moss, variously emerald through to lime green. A shaft of light hit the shining bark of the silver birch trees which acted like a mirror, the reflections causing the interior of the woodland almost to shimmer and breathe.

The lane followed the edge of a loch, and the dogs took to darting in and out of the woodland then racing to the edge of the water and jumping into the clear sparkling water. Elly watched them and was thinking that she might just take a dip too, but something made her turn to her left, away from the dogs. She gasped. Through the thinning trees, on a small natural mound was a large white house with four white pillars and in front of it a small lake half filled with light purple lilies.

Sensing his wife was startled, Tom said gently, "What is it, Elly? You look like you've seen a ghost?"

"It's the house." Elly spoke softly, not moving her gaze.

"What do you mean?" Tom asked.

"I saw this house when I stabbed my hand on the earring; this house flashed through my head!"

"You've probably seen it before — when you were here as a child."

"I don't think so. I never remember coming this side of the campsite. We were only here a couple of days. Dad used to get bored if we stayed put for very long. That's why we had a touring caravan — for touring."

"Nice house, though." Tom said and took Elly's hand and drew her a little further along the lane.

They were no more than thirty feet from the edge of the lily lake, and a track led a short distance around it to an impressive granite gateway from which sturdy metal gates hung slightly open. Just inside of the entrance stood a small woman with a wide smile on her face. On seeing her Barkly raced up to her, wagging his tail furiously and he was quickly joined by Cosmo, keen to be introduced by his new friend. The woman bent down and gently caressed Barkly's head; he responded by pushing his nose into her hand then offering her a paw. Cosmo sat in front of her watching and waiting his turn. She held her hand out towards him, and Cosmo shot to her side keen for all the attention that was on offer.

Tom called, "Sorry! Cosmo come!" But the dog ignored the call, and the woman looked towards Tom and Elly and beckoned them to her. In the bushes to her left, a charm of finches twittered; they seemed to be excited by something.

Standing no more than five feet tall the woman was slightly built, her silver hair up in a soft bun on top of her head. Her skin was not white but lightly tanned, and her eyes were striking, bright and golden almost the same as the dog's. She was wearing an exquisite sari of soft copper and red with a fine-meshed gold head scarf. She continued smiling as Tom and Elly approached.

"I see you have met," she said indicating Barkly who sat beside her like an obedient guard. Her delicate voice sounded Scottish but with an Indian twang.

"Yes," Tom answered. "He appeared and followed us. They've had great fun together. This is Cosmo, by the way. Er, do you live here?" Tom wondered why he'd asked as it seemed blindingly obvious but he felt suddenly lost for conversation. Elly stood beside him, silent, her mouth slightly open, her mind whirring.

"Well, I am sure you would like a refreshing cup of tea." This wasn't what he'd expected, and it came less as a question, more of a non-negotiable statement. The woman turned and walked towards the house, Barkly at her side with Tom, Elly and Cosmo obediently following. No words were spoken as the group walked slowly along the drive to the front of the house with the finches dancing from tree to tree alongside them.

They walked right up the grand steps then under the columned portico to where the two ornately carved, dark wooden doors silently opened before them. The woman turned to Tom and Elly and said in her soft voice, "Welcome to my home." She extended her left arm across her body towards the entrance. Without a word, they walked across the threshold into a hallway lined with paintings, which led to two etched-glass inner doors. These too, opened by themselves revealing a grand inner reception room, circular in shape and with several pairs of double doors set at intervals around its wall. A huge chandelier seemed to float high in the centre of this room. Sunlight from skylights set in a golden dome filtered through its crystal drops to fill the space with a kaleidoscope of moving colour.

From where Tom and Elly stood, just inside the doorway, they could see a broad staircase that followed the curve of the room and rose up to a gallery running the entire circumference of the upper level.

"Shall we go into the day room?" the woman asked, but sought no answer. She led the way around a circular, dark wooden table in the centre of the hall on which sat three silver animals; an elephant, a tiger and, in between them, an impressively large royal stag. As Elly and Tom walked past them the animals' eyes seemed to follow them.

They passed through one of the sets of double doors and into a long room full of light from windows that looked out across sweeping lawns to a shrubbery and tall trees beyond. The woman indicated for them to sit on one of three large sofas and she perched on another opposite them, her back straight and her knees forward, her delicate hands sitting calmly in her lap. Between them was an ornately carved low-standing table on which was set a service of gold-rimmed bone china cups and a silver teapot with steam winding from its spout.

"Well, before tea perhaps it would be appropriate to share names do you think?"

Tom had been thinking not only what a beautiful house this was but also that, for her age, its owner was strikingly beautiful too. He blushed and stuttered, "Y—, yes. Sorry, yes. I'm Tom, and this is my wife, Elly, and you've met Cosmo." Cosmo slightly lifted his head from the deep rug on which he lay close to the woman's feet.

"How lovely to meet you all. My name is Meena, and this is my devoted companion, Barkly."

Tom and Elly flashed each other a look of amazement as Meena told them the dog's name, but they said nothing.

"Tea?" Meena indicated to her guests, who both accepted. "Ah, first flush Darjeeling, my favourite," she said in a happy tone as she poured the golden tea into the delicate handle-less cups and the scent reached her nostrils. She handed one to Elly and then Tom, then she poured herself a cup and softly slurped the first sip. "This is from the finest hand-rolled leaves from the highest tea-gardens of Darjeeling. That is where I am from, but it has been a while since I was there. The tea, you see, reminds me." Her eyes glazed as she seemed lost in memory for a moment.

Elly and Tom slurped their tea, experiencing the pleasure of this delicious, slightly scented drink packed with freshness.

It was as though there was nothing else in the world but this moment with this tea in this beautiful setting and they smiled as they drank.

Tom gazed out of the windows, focussing on the view. He felt it had changed in some way. He looked back into the room, to Elly and the luxurious furnishings then looked again at the view.

"It's changed," he said under his breath. Elly heard the whisper and looked towards the windows but felt compelled to stay as silent as she had since she'd first spotted the house from the lane. Meena continued to sip her tea, watching. She waited until their cups were empty and placed back on the tray.

"I have waited so long for this moment; I never thought it would come. I believe, you see, that you have something that belongs to me. I lost it a very long time ago, and now you are returning it to me."

Meena touched her neck, and from beneath the folds of her sari, she drew out a gold chain on which was suspended what appeared to be a pendant, a small turquoise, blood red and black dome with blue rounded stones hanging from it. Elly gasped as she recognised the small jewel. She felt into her jacket pocket and retrieved the matching earring. She unwrapped it carefully from the tissue, laid it out on her palm and offered it to Meena.

Meena extended her fine finger towards it and as their hands touched Elly saw in her mind a tall, handsome dark-haired man, dressed in traditional Highland clothing and standing on a hillock. The man had a full beard and moustache; on his head he wore a capercaillie-feathered Balmoral bonnet; his Argyll jacket and waistcoat were a rich oatmeal colour and beneath he had a kilt of a dark green plaid. Hanging from the waistband was a silver mounted sporran and tucked in one sock a bejewelled antler with silver trim topped his sgian dubh, secured with a garter flash. On his feet were sturdy, black ghillie's brogues laced up perfectly. The man had a presence about him, a dignified air. It was as though Elly was standing

"You see him, don't you?" said Meena as she took the earring and caressed it. "You too, Tom. You can see my husband, can't you?"

Tom nodded.

"Patrick Campbell-Stewart. I miss him so much." A single bright tear fell from Meena's eye, then she took in a breath and continued.

"You see my dears; the earrings were the very first gift Patrick gave me. Oh, he was so young and dashing, he swept me off my feet the first time I saw him."

Both Elly and Tom who were listening intently found themselves observing the story as though they were in it, live images filling their minds as Meena spoke.

"One fresh, sunny morning a car pulled up on the driveway in front of my grandparents' home — you rarely saw motor vehicles in those days as most of the time you travelled on foot or on small ponies, so this was special. We had an important visitor all the way from Scotland, and my grandfather sent his car to collect him from the newly constructed railway station.

This guest was a businessman, Mr. Alasdair Campbell-Stewart, who owned one of the most important tea producing firms in the country and he was visiting Darjeeling. He was the clan chief of the Campbell-Stewarts, and I will never forget how impressive he looked in his full Highland dress. Accompanying him was his youngest son, Patrick, so young, handsome and tall and also very polite. My grandparents welcomed their guests into their palace. Now, you need to know that my grandparents were the Maharaja and Maharani of their small realm on the mountainside. By then it was an honorific title and didn't mean very much except that it gained them enormous respect. They called their home, a palace, although it was really just a big house with wide verandas sitting on a hill top under the gaze of the Himalayan Mountains. Around the house were beautifully landscaped gardens with wonderful shrubs that seemed to flower year-round and which, especially in the evenings, filled the air with rich scents. I used to play all day in these gardens never tiring of the secret spaces I'd created in the bushes and the stories I told myself there.

"Beyond these gardens, on the wide hillside were the tea plantations. You could see nothing else across the slopes other than tea bushes. Sometimes I would run up and down the rows and get in the way of the pickers. They'd encourage me to help them but my fingers weren't nimble, and I couldn't pay attention to which leaves to pick and which to leave. My grandparents, too, rather frowned on me having anything to do with the pickers. My grandfather said he paid them to do their job, not to play around with me all day. There were snakes and tigers in the plantations too, he said. What would they do if I were attacked or even killed? They would be letting my dear parents down. I didn't tell them that I'd seen tigers and whispered at them to go away and not be shot and that they'd seemed to listen to me.

"I always felt that I was being watched by the guardian mountains; of course, the most impressive one, Kanchenjunga, looked just like a sleeping god and I loved to watch as the sun rose and lit up the mountain ridge, making him glow and seem to come alive."

"Meena, forgive me for interrupting you," said Elly, quietly, "but where were your parents?"

Meena looked past her out through the windows and steadied her breath before answering.

"There'd been an accident when I was very young. My father, in his turn, was learning the tea business and they were away in Delhi. There was a car crash. They both died."

Elly whispered, "I'm so sorry." There was a long, respectful silence until Meena roused herself and clapped her hands lightly.

"Where was I? Oh yes, Patrick. The guests were to stay with us for four weeks and so when my grandfather and Patrick's father were working on their business details, which seemed to be something to do with acquiring more land to plant even more tea, Patrick and I would spend our days walking around the area. He was eighteen, and I was sixteen. Although we were from different parts of the world, there was something we had in common; a love of wide open spaces and being able to walk freely under the mountains. The weather was so good for those weeks too. Patrick had lost his mother to TB, so we shared that sense of there being a hole at the heart of our lives that nothing else seemed to fill."

Tom nodded, knowingly and Meena recognised the reaction, "You, too lost someone when you were a child, Tom?"

Elly reached her hand across to grip Tom's and reassure him that it was safe for him to talk.

"My younger sister. She was fourteen. Hmmm, she was attacked. She was killed." He looked away. Twenty years on and still her innocent face, made up; her hair put up in an outrageous pile on her head and new clothes all ready for partying rose up to haunt him. She had never reached the party; her body found in disarray in local woods two days later.

Meena put her palms together and touched them to her face. Then she held them out to Tom. "I understand," she said.

"Please, please go on. It all sounds so romantic." Tom rallied and focussed all of his attention on this unusual woman's story.

"Well, it was about a week into their visit that my grandmother saw something special was growing between Patrick and I, although she only told me this several months later. She told me that love, although blind to those involved, was quite blatant to those who observed; she had a keen eye and was so perceptive.

"As the month sailed by too quickly, Patrick and I became inseparable. We had so much fun; it was as if this meeting of two young people was always meant to be. Then, two nights before they were due to set off on their long journey back to the Scottish Highlands, my grandmother arranged a reception and dance at the Gymkhana Club.

"The club occupied an impressive wooden building in a prime location overlooking the mountains and valleys. Its interior was breathtaking with a ballroom that was clad in mirrors and with huge chandeliers. The light danced from every surface. The cedar panelling gave off an aroma which was mixed with cigar smoke and ladies' scents. I can smell that even now.

"It was to be a grand affair with visitors attending from all over the Darjeeling region. It was most important to them that they accept the invitation and show their respect for my grandfather and his honoured guests. We were quite formal; the ladies had to sit and wait to be asked to dance. I sat with my grandmother and waited. Clearly, the local boys of my own age were too shy to approach the top table, my grandmother having quite a severe reputation thereabouts. Patrick was looking quite rigid in his dress suit and seemed to be watching the goings on but not paying me any attention at all. I confess I coughed lightly once or twice to try to remind him that I was there and, so to speak, available, but he seemed not to notice. I wondered if I should ever get to dance when suddenly the tempo of the music changed to a beautiful waltz. Patrick turned to me, stood and bowed and offered his hand asking me to dance. I glanced at my grandmother, and she nodded and smiled her approval. As I slipped my hand in his, our first touch, a sensation like I had never experienced tingled through my entire body; he seemed to lift me into the air as if I was gliding above the dance floor. We danced for what seemed like forever; I did not want it to end; I did not want to let go of his hands; I did not want to let that tingle go! Back in my bedroom, I danced round and round, quite dizzy with it all and I knew at that moment that I wanted to be with him for the rest of my life. My grandmother also knew, but then she seemed to know so much.

"The following day grandfather and Patrick's father talked for hours privately in his book-lined study where, behind the closed doors, there were many outbursts of laughter followed by long periods of muffled conversation. Later that day while we all sat around the dining table. Patrick's father stood up and thanked my grandparents for their hospitality and the kindness shown to him and his son during the visit. He was silent for a second and appeared to be deep in thought. I watched as a mixture of emotions flashed across his face and then, with a smile, he looked at his son and declared that it had been decided, indicating to my grandfather and grandma who nodded their heads, that as he needed to leave but return again in twelve months' time, it would be a good idea for Patrick to stay and learn more about the tea business. Patrick flushed bright red and coughed; then he looked at me. Well, you can, of course, imagine, I was thrilled but for dignity's sake managed to hold onto my excitement and merely gave a demure smile. I looked across at my grandmother who was looking back at me, looking deep into my eyes. I knew this was a good thing.

"Formal goodbyes tended to be over quickly. As the car waited to take Patrick's father to the railway station, father and son shook hands vigorously, then Alasdair embraced Patrick and whispered something into his ear. Alasdair looked across to me and smiled. He got into the car and waved and waved until he was out of sight. Patrick returned to his room where he stayed until supper time. I was disappointed, but my grandmother told me that he needed a little time to himself."

"All of this talking is thirsty work." Meena lifted a small brass bell and tinkled it. From the far end of the room, a maid dressed in black with a white apron appeared with a fresh tray of tea and some small cakes. She swapped the trays and left silently. Elly shivered; the tea was definitely real and could not have arrived of its own accord, but that maid had made no sound whatsoever. It was as though she'd passed in and out of the room without using the doors. It was as if she was a ghost. She looked at Tom, but he didn't seem to have noticed and was happily taking one of the madeleines that Meena offered.

"Several weeks passed, and we all settled down into a sort of routine. Patrick accompanied grandfather to the tea gardens where he learned about the methods of producing tea, then to his offices where the more mundane instruction in business procedure was explained. Patrick told me that he rather enjoyed the business side, the pricing and dealing but he found the production side too hot and dusty, and he wasn't too keen on meeting one of the many snakes that lurk in the cool shade under the tea bushes.

"I spent my time with my grandmother helping with her duties as the Maharani. She was grateful for my help, and we got on so well. Now I was more grown-up she told me stories about my mother and father and how they loved to explore; my mother had been something of a free spirit and how I took after her both in appearance and style. On the occasions, she spoke about my mother she would look out over the hills towards the great mountains, losing herself in thought and fond memories of her lost daughter-in-law. She also instructed me in the duties and responsibilities of a devoted wife. On these points, I wasn't so keen, but she insisted on imparting her advice, and I loved her for it in the years that followed."

"Well, that's an amazing story, Meena," Tom said and went to stand up. "We should be getting Cosmo back for his supper now, I think." He looked down at Elly, but she was gazing out of the window. The garden had changed again; the rhododendrons that had been well over when they arrived were now in full bloom.

"No, no!" Meena looked up sharply at him. "I haven't finished telling you how I came here. Please sit. Can I get you anything, any more tea, perhaps?"

"No thank you, but we really should be..." Elly reached up for his arm and pulled Tom back beside her.

"Please go on, Meena. What happened next?" Elly asked, but Tom could tell that her voice was wrong, somehow, that it seemed to come from someone who was not quite awake.

"Well as the weeks passed," Meena closed her eyes and breathed deeply before she continued her tale, "Patrick came to know me better as we spent the afternoons exploring and talking. He told me all about the Highlands of Scotland and in particular the Glen Affric area where he had been born and brought up. He told me about the grand trees, the glens and the streams that could become raging rivers when the rain fell on the hills above. He called them mountains but added that they were nothing like the Himalayas and to me, they are, after all, only hills.

"And he told me about his special place, Creek Waterfall. When he said the name, he breathed in as though he was standing on top of the falls breathing in the cool fresh smell of water tumbling down into an abyss. Immediately I felt that I wanted to visit this place with him; I wanted to inhale the vapour too and look into the depths of the gorge.

"We were to have a day off together. My grandmother bought us tickets for the new train service, the 'toy train' as it became known. Oh, it was such a lovely engine — deep royal blue — and the smell of the steam was almost intoxicating. The route would take us across the vast hills and through the valleys towards the great mountains. I tried hard not to become overexcited. We hardly spoke as we watched the scenery unfold from the carriage windows. I felt I had never travelled in such style, not even in my grandfather's car.

"It was while we waited for the train to arrive for our return journey that Patrick lifted my hand and kissed it. I looked longingly at him, and he took me in his arms and softly kissed my cheek. I wasn't quite sure if my grandmother would have approved of this rather public show of affection, but I didn't stop him as he looked into my eyes and asked if I would do him the honour of becoming his wife. Well, I wanted to act surprised but I couldn't. I threw myself into his arms and kissed him fully on his lips, tears of joy trickling down my face.

"Patrick then pulled away from me and took a step backwards. From his pocket, he produced a small wooden box, on which was embossed an image of the mountains. He presented the box to me and said that these came with eternal love. 'I will formally ask your grandfather tonight.' I opened the box and inside lay a pair of turquoise, red and black earrings with turquoise beads hanging from the rim. At that moment our train arrived."

***

Tom and Elly were standing on a railway station platform, the smell of smoke and steam all around them. In front of them the blue locomotive engine hissed and clunked; the sound of steel on steel, the hum of activity. Elly heard the dog barking first but looking around she could see no dog.

"There it is again," she said to herself. Her attention was once again drawn to the blue steam train as it let off a whistle and steam poured out of the vents. Then there was first deep 'puff' as a great black plume of smoke was pushed from the gleaming chimney. The train whistle was sounded again, and there was another puff, and another and the metal wheels turned slowly. The barking was more persistent, but still, Elly could see nothing in the clouds of thick black smoke. She reached out a hand and found Tom's. They stood unmoving, not coughing nor gasping but unable to move.

"There's a light, look." Tom spoke for the first time in ages. The light was muted, but they walked towards it. Suddenly it was gone, and the darkness was absolute. They laid down together, and the air seemed fresher. The train was chugging into the distance.

"Tom, Elly are you there?" Elly opened her eyes; still the absolute darkness. The voice came again quite close by, "Tom, Elly are you there?" Then there was a scratching sound followed by a whine and more barking. She felt so tired and closed her eyes again.

Bernard Willis shone his torch along the landing and saw a door ahead of him, which he was certain was where the barking was coming from. As he came close, there was frantic scratching and loud sniffs as the dog scented his presence.

"Is that you, Cosmo?" He whispered. "Have you got Tom and Elly in there with you, lad?" There came a responding series of barks. Bernard called their names for a third time before he slowly turned the door handle.

Cosmo could not contain himself; he flew out onto the landing, raced up and down a few times and jumped at Bernard's back.

"Shhh, lad. Calm down and show me where they are."

Cosmo led him into a dark room that was thick with smoke, but the dog wasn't keen to go too far and wrapped himself around Bernard's legs, staying as close as possible for comfort and support. Bernard swept his torch around the room and thought he could pick out a large bed by the furthest wall. He was certain there were figures lying on it.

"Tom, Elly is that you?" He whispered rather than shouting. The room was cold beyond measure, and he felt as though he was walking into a morgue. The smoke swirled round him again. He pointed the torch at the floor to find his way forward and could see that several of the floorboards had rotted through leaving gaping holes right through to the hall below. He wondered if he should retreat and call for help, more lights perhaps, but that could take hours, and they may have no time left. They may already be dead. No, he wouldn't believe that; he must find out what had happened, then he could phone for an ambulance and support if he needed it. There was a great deal of smoke but seemingly no fire, and this didn't smell like a house fire; it reminded Bernard of something long gone, like this house, but he couldn't place it.

He was standing no more than a foot or two inside the door and could see the wall to his left clearly. The floor seemed sound on that side, and he reached out to use the wall as his guide. He could see various items of furniture as he came to them and he managed to work his way round until he was standing a few feet from the largest bed he had ever seen. The air was clearer now, and he could see two people lying side-by-side, holding hands.

"Tom? Elly?" He asked quietly now believing that he had come too late and they were indeed dead. As he stepped forward towards them, having fully prepared himself for the worst, Cosmo leapt from his side and pounced onto the bed and licked at their faces, turning from one to the other, pawing at them, scrabbling at the counterpane. It shredded in his claws. When his owners didn't respond, he stood at the bottom of the bed and let out two loud barks and a long howl.

Elly stirred first, opening her eyes then squeezing them shut again against the light from Bernard's torch.

"Cosmo, what's the fuss?" she asked quietly. Cosmo leapt onto her and licked her nose. She pushed him off and sat up.

"Tom, Tom wake up! What's happened? Wake up!" She shook his shoulder, and Cosmo transferred his attention. Tom stirred and said something about a train, then said, "Where's Meena? Did she get on the train?"

Bernard had been about to introduce himself and suggest they get the hell out of the old house but at the mention of the name 'Meena' his blood ran cold. He shook off the thoughts that rattled through his head and asked instead if they were all right.

They looked towards him squeezing their eyes in the sudden bright light.

"Who are you?" Tom asked. "I can't see you."

"Ah, sorry." Bernard shone the torch towards the floor. "My name's Bernard, but I need to know whether to call an ambulance for you. First things first. So how do you feel?"

"I think I'm OK," replied Elly. "Tom?"

"Yes, I'm fine though I'm not sure why we're lying on a bed. My head's a little confused."

"Yeah, kind of muzzy," Elly added.

Sensing the immediate panic was over, Bernard perched on the edge of the bed and asked them how they'd come to be in the old estate house.

"We were walking along the lane and met Meena. She invited us in, served us tea and started to tell us about her life. Then we were on a station platform seeing her and her fiancé off, and now we are on a bed in the dark with a stranger asking us if we are OK!" Tom explained.

Bernard realised that the couple were very confused about things.

"Look, I'll just put the torch onto solid light mode and lay it at the foot of the bed, and we'll be able to see each other." He fiddled with the torch for a moment and muttered, 'technology don't you just love it?' Suddenly their end of the room was flooded with light.

Bernard could clearly see the couple with their dog, wisps of smoke still swirling around their heads and he could also smell the smoke; then he understood what Tom had said. "Train, yes it's the smell of a steam train." He hadn't meant to say it so loudly. Tom looked at him and said, "Can you smell it too?" Bernard nodded in surprise.

"So, who exactly are you, Bernard?" Elly wasn't ready for any more confusion. She felt slightly adrift as though she were experiencing several realities at once and her body was not quite solid, not quite her own.

"I'm Bernard Willis, and I have the small hotel in the village. You two were booked in last night, but you didn't turn up. I knew from my conversation with Tom that you had been camping at Tall Trees, so we checked out your tent. Clearly, you hadn't been back to it. You'd been seen walking up the track towards the Creek Waterfall, which is quite a dangerous place, so when you didn't arrive, we got worried and decided to search there for you."

Tom said, a little brusquely, "But we're not due to stay with you until the 16th, that's tomorrow."

Bernard looked at the couple and replied, gently, "I'm sorry, but today is the 17th, and you left the campsite on the 15th."

In the silence, the air cleared completely, and Cosmo lay between the couple licking first Elly's hand then Tom's.

"Are you saying that we have been missing for two days?" Ellie asked, uncertainly.

Bernard said softly, "Yes."

"But how, I mean...how is that possible? All we did was have a cup of tea with this Meena woamn. This is too confusing." Tom was becoming slightly irritated, feeling that this was part of an elaborate hoax. "You're having a laugh! Who set you up to do this? What's going on? Where's Meena and why is the house in this state?"

Again Bernard spoke softly, anxious not to increase their anxiety.

"Look we need to leave this house. Let's get you to the hotel, and we can talk more about what has or has not happened; get you fed and reunite you with your belongings. The room is all set up ready. Are you OK with that?"

They could do nothing but trust him and agree.

With Cosmo by their side, they followed Bernard with his torch safely out of the bedroom and around the long gallery, down the stairs and into the large hallway. Tom stopped and looked around in the dim light.

"The table with the stag and tiger; where is it?"

Bernard swung his torch across the room's expanse. The space was empty.

"Look, let's just leave, shall we? My truck is on the lane, and you two need a dram." Bernard replied.

Tom grabbed at Bernard's sleeve and pulled him around to face them.

"How did you know we were in the house?"

"I thought I saw smoke coming out of the chimney stack above the room you were in." They didn't speak again until they arrived at the hotel.

***

The double-fronted, Victorian Glen Hotel was a family run concern, popular with residents and locals alike. It offered great food, real ales and a warm welcome to dogs. By the time the truck pulled up outside Tom and Elly were looking forward to relaxing in a jacuzzi, followed by a slap-up meal and several drams. They suddenly felt very hungry indeed.

As they stepped down from the truck, they were greeted by a tall woman who said in a soft Scottish accent, "Oh! Thank God, you're safe my dears." She hugged them both. "Come, come the fires are lit. I'll go put the kettle on."

"I think they need something a little stronger than tea, Effie. We'll go into the lounge; it'll be quiet in there at this time of day." Bernard replied.

He led his guests into a cosy lounge where there were two comfortable sofas and a couple of bucket chairs. A fire roared in the hearth, the logs hissing and spitting and the flames leapt high into the flue. He suggested they sit next to the fire. As they passed him closely, Bernard briefly caught the smell of steam trains, but he didn't say anything. He needed to settle the bewildered couple and listen to their strange experience. Cosmo found a comfortable spot on a rug in front of the fire and fell instantly asleep, twitching and waffling as he dreamed. Occasionally, one eye would open and settle on his owners.

Effie came in carrying a tray with a plateful of freshly made sandwiches, a pot of tea, several cups and four tumblers half-filled with golden liquor. Famished, Tom and Elly made short work of the food and tea. Seeing Cosmo's nose twitching then sniffing vigorously, Effie lowered a small plate of beef that she'd made up specially for him. He sat to attention and when Elly said, "Yes, Cosmo," he swept his tongue round the food in one quick movement, swallowed, belched and curled himself back onto his rug.

Now, with their whisky tumblers warming in their hands, Tom

and Elly relaxed and felt able to recount what had happened to them with Bernard and Effie filling in the background.

"We met a lady wearing a sari in the lane," started Elly. "She led us up to the white house on the mound with her dog and said her name was Meena."

"Yes, Meena. There's quite a story about Meena." Bernard interrupted. "She was the wife of the last Laird of this estate, Patrick Campbell-Stewart. The story goes that the two of them were introduced when Patrick was in India with his father."

"Darjeeling, actually," Elly added.

Bernard gave her a quizzical look; Elly explained, "She told us all about growing up there."

Bernard had decided not to show his doubts about Elly's state of mind and hoped all would be explained when he told them the truth of the local history. He went on.

"Long before this building became a hotel it was home to the estate manager and his family who served the Campbell-Stewart family around about a hundred and ten years ago. The Laird then, was Patrick and his young wife was Meena."

Elly gasped. "But how can that be? We met her today. We had tea with her!"

"The experience you had was two days ago, my dear. Some strange things have taken place over the years, and it would seem that you'll be adding to the list." Effie rocked back in her chair.

"But she was as clear as day, as solid as you are sitting there, I swear it. I touched her hand." Elly insisted and was starting to feel distressed. Tom put his arm around her and shook his head silently.

Bernard went to a book shelf and selected a dark green, leather-bound book. Opening it, he flicked through several pages and passed it to Elly.

"Ah, yes," he said. "There it is, not the best photo but look at it closely."

Elly took the old book and held it between for Tom to see. On the page was an old sepia photograph, showing a large white house with four pillars supporting a portico. Standing in front of the house were two people and a dog.

"Tom, it's her, Meena, younger but it is her and, oh my god, it's Patrick!" Elly spoke so quietly.

"The dog, look at the dog! Barkly, I don't believe it, Barkly!" Tom pointed at the photograph and looked into Elly's face, sharing their disbelief. "But how?" Tom added weakly, feeling as though the earth beneath him was shaking and that he had no hold on what might be real.

Elly started to cry, overwhelmed by a sense of loss and confusion. What had happened to their happy holiday? Where had they lost two days and how come it had all felt so real?

Effie looked across at Bernard who shrugged his shoulders. This wasn't the first time. Effie went and got a fresh bottle of whisky and refilled the glasses.

"Come on, my dears. This will help you relax. You've had a shock and no mistake."

Tom hugged Elly to him until she regained control and sniffed and sipped at her glass. The golden liquid ran down her throat in a warming stream and seemed to carry on right down into her legs. This feeling, at least, she knew, and she let it take her into a safer place for a moment.

"Tom?" Bernard checked to see if his guest was ready for more. Tom nodded. "You met the dog, too?"

"It found us and took to Cosmo, so it came with us. It barked a great deal, so we christened it 'Barkly'. Then when we met Meena, she told us that was its name. And that is pretty weird."

"The strange thing is," Bernard replied, "that we've heard several visitors asking who owns a similar dog. They all say that the dog simply joined them on their walks, particularly if they were going to the Creek Waterfall. We've never found an owner who's reported a dog gone walkabout."

"You should tell them the rest of it, Bernard." Effie said, realising that soon there would be a steady stream of guests booking in and the dinners to be started.

"Yes, right then," said Bernard. "As you know, Meena and Patrick lived in the large white house, 'Affric House' to be exact. They were deeply in love and shared the duties of estate life together. They had no children and, in fact, were the end of the Campbell-Stewart family line. They liked to think they made the estate workers and all hereabouts their family. So, it is said that they would invite the whole community to the house for regular gatherings. They would share a large spread of food and organise games and fun for everyone. Times were hard for most, so it was seen as a generous gesture. They were popular folk.

"Sadly their lives would change forever. The story goes that they were out walking one day up at the Creek Waterfall, when Patrick slipped and fell. When the alarm went off the estate workers rushed to the waterfall and at great risk to themselves they got to him. He was tied in a makeshift rope stretcher and hauled up, but he died in Meena's arms at the top of the waterfall. Meena was inconsolable.

"Following the funeral, she could be seen walking with her beloved Barkly towards the waterfall. One day she never returned, and her remains have never been located. It is believed that she also fell or jumped off the waterfall. Why do they believe it was at the waterfall? Well, her dog refused to leave the top slabs. He just lay there barking and whimpering. Staff from the estate took food to him, but he wouldn't eat. Then one day he too had disappeared, and again no remains were ever found.

"The house was left empty and with no heirs and seemingly a complicated set up over ownership down through the generations, there it still remains, slowly falling down.'

"But the house was beautiful, full of light and furniture and there was a maid who brought the..." Elly stopped to think, "But Meena was old, at least, older than the time you're describing, and she still had the dog. And how come we ended up in a bedroom completely unconscious but smelling of steam trains?

I was there on the platform, I know I was. I don't understand. None of this makes any sense at all."

"Yes," said Bernard. "This time it is different. People meet the dog, but I can't think anyone has had tea with Meena before. I wonder what is different about you two." He looked at them quite harshly as though they may have elaborated on what was, after all, a fairly well-known folk tale in the area.

Tom suddenly said, louder than he'd meant to, "The earring, the gold earring Elly found at the top of the falls!"

"What do you mean, Tom?" Bernard could see no relevance to this at all.

Tom explained all that had happened to Elly but didn't mention the scream that he thought he'd heard and dismissed as his own internal fear playing tricks.

"But I gave the earring to Meena, she took it, don't you remember?" She felt in her jacket pockets. They were definitely empty.

★★★

As the evening's guests started to drift into the lounge, Effie took Tom, Elly, and Cosmo to their room and suggested she bring them up a bit of supper later. She could see that Elly was in no state to make herself presentable in the dining room.

Tom was asleep before the last of the day's light had left the sky, but Elly kept turning the events of the last few days over and over in her head. What was it about her that seemed to channel these forces; how could she keep experiencing other people's lives like this. First, it had been the German airman on Cumbrae and now Meena. Most of the time she felt perfectly normal, young and fit with an ordinary job and a loving husband. She wondered if she should talk to someone about it. Tom didn't seem concerned. He was so easy going, simply taking each day as it arrived, working his way through it, ticking life's little boxes, turning over and sleeping soundly. He had such an ally in Cosmo. She thought of Molly and wondered how Helen was getting along. There'd been no messages so that must all be fine. She missed her Mol, though. Mol would have been beside her now, nosing her head beneath her hand ignoring the 'no dogs on the beds' rule, sensing all Elly's anxieties and telling her it would all be fine. Things would work out; they always did.

Elly must have slept then because the next thing she heard was a knock at the door and Bernard coming in with the biggest breakfast tray she'd ever seen.

"Will I just let Cosmo out in the garden?" he enquired. Cosmo was already out of the room, down the stairs and barking at the kitchen door. "Not that way, young man!" Bernard was right behind him and led him out of a side door into a beautiful autumn morning.

Their farewells were brief. Effie gave Tom and Elly a packed lunch for their journey home, and she hugged Elly tightly and whispered to her, "Travel safely, my dear. Visit us any time; you are both so much a part of the richness of this part of the world; it's almost as if you belong. Bless you, both." Her sharp blue eyes moistened, she put her head down and went back indoors. Bernard echoed the return invitation and wished them well.

***

Elly was rushing around their home trying to locate her car keys, already late for work. Since returning from Glen Affric, she felt as though she had a weight on her mind. It was as if she couldn't seem to find the fun in anything. The dogs' antics would make her smile but no longer laugh out loud. In the evenings she'd taken to curling up on the sofa with a book, Molly now much recovered tucked in alongside her. She thought that Tom had forgotten all about the holiday and seemed to have picked up working life just where it had left off. Elly could not get the image of Meena out of the front of her mind; it was as though she were accompanied everywhere by her touch and her scent.

She was wrong about Tom. He was mostly worried about Elly who had seemed to withdraw into herself unable to rationalise the events. He had tried to lay it to one side, but it was niggling away at him; he didn't feel he could burden his wife any further with his worries, so he tried to concentrate on work and the practical things in life.

Frantic that her keys weren't in the house for some inexplicable reason, Elly's shoulders started to shake, and she knew she was about to start crying. It kept happening to her, this feeling of being challenged all the time by the slightest thing. She picked up her mobile and started to locate Tom's number but before it could ring there was a knock at the door. She cancelled the call, wiped her face and pulled herself together. The postman was on the step with a parcel to be signed for. She wasn't expecting anything, so it must be something Tom had ordered. As she laid the parcel on the hall table, she spotted her keys where they'd fallen down beside her wellington boots. She looked in the mirror, pushed her hands through her hair and hoped the red rings around her eyes might have gone by the time she got to work.

Tom was home first that evening and having walked the dogs and organised a meal; he sat down at his laptop to catch up on his emails. Amongst the usual rubbish, there was one from beandef@glenhotel.co.uk that didn't seem to be simply a follow up offer of a weekend break for two in darkest winter. Tom double-clicked.

Dear Tom and Elly, thought you'd be interested in the attached articles from the local paper.
Hope all is well with you both.
Kind regards
Bernard and Effie

Tom clicked on the attachment just as Elly came through the door. She kissed his forehead and spotted the headline on the screen.

Hundred Year Mystery of Missing Lady Solved

"From Bernard and Effie. They thought we'd be interested." Tom said. "Too right!" Elly replied. They read the article together.

As we reported three weeks ago, cave explorers studying the geology of the Creek Waterfall gorge in Glen Affric encountered a grizzly scene.

On a ledge deep within a cave at the bottom of the waterfall, they located human remains, which they believed to be the those of Meena Campbell-Stewart. The last Laird's wife disappeared after his death in a tragic fall at the location over a hundred years ago.

The existence of the body together with a smaller set found beside her, believed to be those of her dog, was reported to the procurator fiscal.

Subsequent examination has now been able to confirm the identity of Mrs. Campbell-Stewart and her dog, which was called, Barkly.

A brief service took place last Friday at the Campbell-Stewart family graves where both sets of remains were buried alongside Patrick Campbell-Stewart. Several local people were in attendance including the local hotel-keeper, Mr. Bernard Willis. He commented, 'This burial concludes a hundred-year-old or more mystery. It has brought back together a couple who were deeply in love and puts to rest the souls of Patrick, Meena and, of course, their dog, Barkly. May they now all rest in peace.'

It is understood that there was no family.

Elly felt the weight of the last few weeks lift from her shoulders;

she wept and laughed at the same time, and Tom slammed his laptop lid down and nearly lifted her off her feet, dancing her around the kitchen.

"Ghosts, Elly. It was just ghosts!"

"Ah! Nearly forgot there's a parcel in the hall. What have you been buying?" Elly asked, playfully.

"Nothing. I saw it there and thought it must have been yours," Tom replied, going through to collect it.

Elly tore at the neat brown-paper wrapping. Inside was a tiny hand-crafted wooden box. Embossed on the lid of the box was a scene that Elly instantly recognized. It was a sunrise over Kanchenjunga. She slowly opened the box. A hand-written note sat on top of the contents, its beautiful copperplate reading:

'Reunited, at last, thank you, M'.

Elly sat heavily on a kitchen chair. Beneath the note was a pair of gold earrings enamelled in turquoise, red and black, turquoise discs hanging from the rims. Elly took the earrings out of the box and held them up for Tom to see. As she did, she was sure she heard a distant 'bark, bark, bark'. Cosmo ran to her, bounced off her knee and replied with his own, 'bark, bark, bark'.

DRAW YOURSELF A PICTURE
AND STEP IN!

The telephone rang in her office, "Seaview Gallery can I help?" Ruby answered. "Give me a moment while I check my diary." Feeling slightly foolish, as this client wanted to visit in the next hour or so, she pencilled in the time she could expect her visitor. Picking up the handset she said, "Yes darling, but of course, eleven-thirty suits me just fine, see you then, bye-bye." She replaced the shiny black Bakelite receiver onto its brass cradle on top of the antique telephone.

Ruby lived with her husband Adam, a professional percussionist a short walk from breathtaking sea views, in the northern Scottish Highlands. Her studio faced north-west and captured masses of natural light through the enormous, floor to ceiling windows. Proud in the centre of her studio was her beloved easel and, standing some seven feet tall, it was able to hold securely in place the large, five-foot by four-foot handmade canvases. The oil paints were neatly, but seemingly, randomly, laid out on her workstation and a whole range of used, wet oil paints sat like small mountains on the wooden surface. Brushes of all sizes stood to attention in recycled jam and coffee jars; for the larger brushes, old stoneware storage jars were used as these were more stable and held lots of brushes. The smell of turps, linseed and oil paint reminded visitors of their colourful old art rooms at school. That was before the invention of computers and 'CAD' designs. Standing in strategic areas around the space were large leafy plants bathed in the light from the window, a sense of the tropics came to mind. All in all, the studio was a peaceful and pleasant environment in which to be creative.

Ruby returned to her studio and continued to work on her latest oil painting. Selecting a generous scoop of ultramarine, she applied it heavily to the canvas, the mark producing a sense of depth in the multicoloured seascape. She sighed with satisfaction. Then she selected phthalo green and phthalo blue, together with a hint of titanium white which blended lightly — not completely — creating a beautiful turquoise and deep green-blue, the white producing a translucency suggesting shallow water. The skyscape was a rich mix of soft blue with wispy, white clouds and the hint of rays of sunshine. The foreground contained lime-green seaweed, and by introducing a highlight of silver and gold, the shore vegetation was suddenly vibrant, mobile and alive. Ruby was quite content with the result. She continued.

The gallery doorbell rang. So absorbed with her paintings, Ruby had lost track of time; a brief irritation washed over her at being disturbed, but this was quickly replaced by her usual joyful manner when she remembered who was calling. Answering the door, Ruby smiled generously at her client her client, "Henry, how lovely to see you again, please come in out of the cold."

Henry Jones entered the large and welcoming reception hall where he couldn't help but marvel at all of the delightful, aged photographs of Ruby's long-passed family, reflecting a very different time. Removing his smart, Harris Tweed jacket, he hung it on a coat hook and followed Ruby into the inner hallway.

Ruby said, "It's so good to see you after such a long time, I hope that life has treated you well?"

Henry replied, "Yes so-so, thank you for asking. I'm so eager to see your latest work. I've been following your progress posts on your web pages and social media — my how things change. I recall you having to send me a photograph in the post each time you had a new piece, just like that first piece I purchased from you. I love that painting, always have, it takes me to a special place."

Henry had purchased several originals over the years; he was probably the only other person who completely appreciated and fully understood the significance of Ruby's work.

Ruby noticed that her client was becoming slightly emotional. So as not to dwell on matters Ruby said, "Let's go into my exhibition gallery, lots to show you there." Henry agreed and followed. As they walked along a brightly lit corridor, Henry became aware of the haunting sound of Indian folk music. Bamboo instruments, deep round drum sounds, trickling water — or rain song — seeds cascading within long bamboo stems, gentle bamboo whistles all played the rhythms accompanying and weaving melody through the complex, yet pure, song. It was a soothing and uplifting sound and complemented the sense of creativity present in this warm, homely place.

Ruby showed Henry into a large room with a high ceiling and no windows. The interior of the room wasn't brightly lit which gave the individually illuminated oil paintings a grand presence, each hanging in its own place against the soft, rich, cream-coloured walls. Each piece took the viewer to a new and wonderful visual experience, the spaces between each painting just enough to link them all harmoniously. Henry breathed in pleasantly as he stepped into this most impressive space. However, it was not the completed works of art that caught his attention first. He could see clearly through into the neighbouring studio space which seemed to be flooded with a rich and evocative light. This light appeared to brighten in the moment he cast his gaze into the interior of the working studio. Standing proudly, and almost to attention, on the tall easel was Ruby's latest work. Henry had followed the progress of this piece with great interest.

Ignoring all of the hung work, Henry approached the large glass door that separated the hanging gallery from the studio space. Without asking, he gently pushed the door open and walked straight into Ruby's studio. Ruby looked on, a little taken aback, but she knew instinctively what was happening as she had seen this sort of reaction on many occasions. She knew that when a person finds something that they immediately connect with, there is rarely anything else that can distract them from committing themselves to their goal. They are sucked into the moment. It was clear that Henry had emotionally connected to Ruby's latest work.

Henry stood in front of the large and impressive scene, swaying to and fro as if seeming to hear the gentle movement of the sea, all the while matching the rhythm of the beautiful and soothing Indian music that was filling the studio space. Ruby simply watched, as this was for her a truly wonderful moment.

Her work had struck a chord with another and was igniting their sensibilities; a passionate affair had started, there was no need for any more words for the time being.

For several minutes Ruby watched Henry stare at the unfinished work in silence. Eventually, she said in a soft tone, "I think I should make the coffee, darling, and leave you for a while." There was a sort of acknowledgment from Henry's shoulders, but he didn't take his gaze from the painting.

Ruby left the studio and went to the other end of the house. The teas and coffees were never made in the gallery as the sound of a boiling kettle, or the chinking of bone china against bone china could shatter a precious moment, so all utilities were carried out, out of earshot.

As Ruby was making the refreshments, her telephone began to ring. Leaving the kitchen, she answered the call from a close friend wanting to discuss a dinner party that was to take place in four weeks' time. Normally, with clients present Ruby would express her apologies and tell the caller she would return their call. On this occasion, however, Ruby was confident Henry was quite happy acquainting himself with her work and so she started a conversation regarding the dinner arrangements. As these arrangements do, the details took some time.

Pulling a note pad from his pocket, Henry wrote,

Dear Ruby, I love this piece and will have it on completion. I attach a cheque.
So sorry I couldn't wait for you to return, something pressing you understand. Forgive my silent exit but know that I am very happy and contented with this beautiful work of art.
Kindest regards Henry.

He placed the note and cheque onto the floor in front of the easel. Stepping closer to the canvas he lifted his small note pad and drew a picture frame. The sides weren't straight, in fact it looked like an oblong box, but in a familiar way it really was a picture frame. He roughly sketched the image in front of him and placed a matchstick figure on the edge of the water. Henry then placed the paper in front of the painting and put his right forefinger onto it within the frame. After a second or two his finger appeared to be absorbed into the sketch and the paper itself began to meld into the canvas. In a flash of light, Henry was gone. All that remained in front of the canvas was the note and the payment. At the same moment the smart Harris Tweed jacket hanging in the lobby also vanished.

Ruby had completed her telephone conversation. Hot water was poured into the cafetière and left to stand for a while. Placing a selection of home-baked shortbread biscuits onto an ornate, porcelain side plate, then placing two bone china teacups and saucers onto a sturdy mahogany tray, together with the coffee pot, Ruby walked back to her studio. Pushing the door open with her back she said, "So sorry darling, a friend's dinner party arrangements you understand, sorry I took so long." Ruby stopped mid-sentence as she looked inside her studio and found it to be empty. At first, she didn't see the paper on the floor. Placing the tray carefully onto a side table, she called, "Henry darling, are you there? Coffee's ready." There was no reply. Looking around the interior of the studio then glancing back into the gallery space, it was clear that these spaces were empty. Nonetheless, she scrutinised them closely, a puzzled look on her face. Ruby called Adam and asked, "Did you hear Henry leave, sweetie?"

Adam said, "Who? I didn't hear anyone arrive!"

Ruby said, "You usually hear the vehicles arrive, don't you? Did you not hear his?"

Adam, entering the studio, looked at Ruby a little puzzled, then said, "Nothing came down the drive darling, I would have heard it. I certainly would have heard a car leaving, I mean the gravel is quite noisy!"

Ruby returned to her studio, and a silly thought occurred to her — could Henry have passed out in a corner somewhere?

"Adam darling, would you be kind enough to go and look in the loo, you never know?" Adam dutifully left.

Meanwhile, Ruby scanned the studio once more; then she saw the notepaper on the floor. Picking it up she realised there was another slip of paper — a cheque. The cheque was made out to Ruby to the value of twenty-thousand pounds; it was dated ten days earlier and was for more than double her usual price. For a second she could barely stand, then, gathering her thoughts, she read the note again. She called to Adam, who had made a thorough search of the downstairs cloakroom.

A painting is a portal which allows the viewer to be transported into another world or realm. The question is:

'Are they aware of this fact?'

For its creator it is an extension of themselves, every mark made is a part of their heart and soul, every shade of colour reflects their inner self. The making of each mark has meaning; it is another line in the painting's unique story. The key is to make each line count, give every mark value, bring the work to life.

Stepping through the portal the individual begins a journey of discovery, a journey that is enriched by the interaction with the artist's emotional brush strokes and mark-making. Both artist and viewer will have differing encounters, but the two journeys will be closely linked and grow together, eventually evolving into the complete picture.

And so, Henry Jones begins his journey.

Like a gannet being carried on warm thermals, Henry enters this painterly realm. Flying high across the colourful picture he can see many details both below and above him. Of course, this realm is not yet complete but what is there is beautiful and peaceful, his perfect place to be.

Unlike the actual painting which is contained by sides and edges and frames, on the inside of his painting there are no such constraints, no boundaries, just like a small universe it simply goes on and time has little or no effect.

As Henry continues to glide over the vista, he marvels at the visual stimuli he is absorbing — colour, texture; life and energy. It was his and he would make the very best of it.

He is also aware of sounds, soft music all around, beautifully composed and choreographed melodies entwine creating audible colour and texture. Bamboo instruments softly play, pushing and pulling to the gentle wave motion, feeling the musical movement, then the sea responding.

Haunting, barely audible whistles blow in unison with the invisible bird song further filling the musical score. Brush strokes on a snare drum build up then soften together with the gently swaying sea grasses that grow just under the surface of the water. It is not just the sounds from the surface that can be heard, quite the opposite; Henry can hear the astonishing variety of sounds emanating from under the surface of the water. The whole painting is a collaboration of visual and audio sensations. Usual senses are not so usual in this realm.

Henry comes to a gentle landing area where soft, warm sand hugs his bare feet. He sees a large boulder which could have been designed just for him. He sits in his natural chair and watches the evolving image. Quiet tears fall from his eyes, only to be caught and absorbed by his comfortable chair, which seems to wrap Henry in the finest Alpaca wool. He is completely safe and at peace.

***

Following the abrupt disappearance of Henry from Ruby's studio, matters continued almost as normal. The encounter with Henry simply faded from the front of Ruby's mind and she thought no more about the visit. The payment for the painting was cashed without any issues. However, deep in a corner of her mind, Ruby knew something was not quite as it should be. Both she and Adam had initially attempted to make contact with Henry but all leads went cold. They tried to trace him via his bank, nothing. It had occurred to them that previous encounters had also been somewhat odd. A call from Henry, an image, or later an email, was then sent, resulting in a purchase. There was no lead either to be got from his email address. And so, although Henry was there, he was also not there!

Ruby felt that under the circumstances she should continue to finish off the work purchased by Henry. Normally she would have two or three paintings on the go at any given time, but this was different. And so making her usual preparations, Ruby selected her favoured music for that moment, waited a while until the natural light was just right, then picked up her brush and continued.

***

Henry looks forward to this moment when he can be present as his realm is filled with more painterly detail. He wonders what colours will be selected, how thick and textured the next mark will be. His excitement builds.

Henry becomes aware that more work is about to take place because the music he has been listening to suddenly changes. Today it is jazz, an upbeat tempo with lots of strong drum beats tailing off before an explosion of what seem to be four instruments playing slightly different tunes but all blending together to form a structured and exciting musical riff. Ruby paints with the same enthusiasm; a deep ridge of copper highlighting several rocks that are appearing out of the shallow water, a hint of lime-green on the now exposed rock, then a touch of gold and white acting as highlights where the rocks are suddenly touched by a shaft of sunlight.

Henry is enthralled to be present when his painting is being so skilfully and imaginatively worked on. Ruby has no idea that she has an audience. If she had looked more closely at the detail in her work, she would have seen a tiny mark that she was not responsible for. She would have seen what appeared to be a boulder that looked like a chair and would have also seen the owner of this painting sitting comfortably, watching and listening. But there again, who does look so closely at the finer details contained in a painting?

The latest strokes having been completed, it is time for more drying to take place and so Henry decides to investigate another painting that he has always wanted to enter. It was an early purchase of Ruby's work.

Taking out his note pad Henry once again sketches a picture frame, this time drawing a huge wave, a wave that fills the pencilled frame. Putting his finger onto the image Henry is, once more, absorbed into the picture.

Travelling between these paintings is quite simple. All of Ruby's pieces of artwork are closely related; like all other artists' work, they are linked and share the essence of the creator who made the marks on the canvases.

As Henry glides through into 'The Wave', he can hear a change in the sound. Cymbals are being softly played using felt beaters, a sound like shhhhhhshh which becomes more intense as Henry travels closer. Henry can feel pressure around him; he can taste the misty, salty seawater; still, the sound around him builds up, the sense of excitement heightening as Henry gets closer. Then the shushing begins to fracture, changing to the sound of cracking wood against the metal rim of a drum, the pressure continues to rise, his excitement almost boiling over. Then, with a loud crash of the cymbals being struck perfectly together, the wave breaks, a crescendo of music and movement fills his heart. Henry is safely inside the wave, observing this wonderful event, pure joy coursing through him. Rushing water is all around, cymbals ring out with sparkling energy, then the wave softens, and the watery bamboo sound begins once again as the waters caress the pebbles on the beach and turn to soft rainbow-colored bubbles.

Henry turns back into the wave. This time he wants to look through the water, feel the weight of the clear salty sea; he wants to be part of the crescendo of light, water, and energy, invigorating, breathtaking; he never wants it to end. He begins to move to the rising rhythms and, sensing the sounds, he stretches out his arms, dips his fingertips into the soft, warm water which sends tingling through his body and, as he starts to move slowly, the movements become a slow swaying dance. To his delight, the waters surrounding him start to move in the same way, clear water curving and bending to Henry's dance. A smile appears within the deep aquamarine water.

Other creatures become curious; a giant trigger fish with its tightly pinched upper lips turns to one side in order to give its huge revolving eye a better view of the evolving performance. With its tiny fins moving to the same rhythms the trigger fish swoops and sways when, all of a sudden, hundreds of different fish including a huge variety of Spanish dancers join in. Jellyfish gently fold and shimmer; a whole rainbow of colours glisten and sparkle moving through their translucent bodies like pulses of electricity.

Each wave builds up to a crescendo and crashes with the smash of metallic sound, only to be gently pulled back and built up once again — the soft cymbal tones urging to be released. The sound of joy and laughter is all around; everything is moving as one. Other laughter joins in. Henry recognises them: here are friends, their distinctive voices sending him off into another bout of hysterical joy.

Another wave crashes then starts to rebuild, and Henry wonders what it would be like to visit deeper water. He is aware that he is now travelling within his bubble further out to sea and he can see the aquamarine water alter colour to turquoise, and then to ultramarine, the rich blueness created by depth. He looks into this new world, and the sound of a deep, song bowl resonates all around him. Shadows of giant whales move across the vista, elongated trumpet shaped rays of light touching them. The sound becomes a joyful whale song, which gives Henry goose bumps all over. In that moment, Henry understands their ancient story and weeps. He becomes certain that all is now well; the Giants are content and happy in this realm.

Henry decides that he has had such a wonderful time that he will return to his boulder seat on his unfinished beach and rest for a while before his next adventure.

***

Henry Jones was a kind man, but he never stood out from the crowd. This was by choice as he was a successful international businessman with a wealth that was breathtaking and his altruism was equally so. His preferred means of living was in quiet privacy; he had never married and was the last member of his extended family. Henry employed trusted people who in turn kept Henry out of notice from almost all aspects of his business; and, more than that, they assured his life was treated with dignity and reserve. He had several close friends who respected his lifestyle and, because of that, the friendships became life-long. There were no flash cars; there was no flash anything. His staff simply knew that they were employed by a tender and generous man. His only passion was to collect art. He loved to follow and invisibly sponsor new talent, taking great delight in watching the artists grow and prosper. Where it was appropriate, he would facilitate a helping hand as he found some of the art world too stiff and pompous to give assistance to talent, particularly if that talent was not from 'their' house!

"Art should be shared, not saved for the few!" He would say in private.

Not one of those who had been helped knew about his kindness. Henry would simply say, "Well, they would never ask, and so I will always give." It was a simple philosophy.

Ruby was one of these artists. Henry recognised almost instantly that she had great artistic talent and integrity, and so, unknown to her, he began silently to open doors. This was the start of his love affair with Ruby's work, a love affair, for him that would last forever.

***

The sound of jazz filling the air informs Henry that Ruby is about to resume the finishing touches to his painting — the final marks that would be applied to the work. He is in his garden, a garden which, in the picture, is out of sight. In fact, there were many things within this painting that were out of sight. For example, Henry finds that he is able to visit friends and that they too have special places where they find tranquillity. The strange thing is that all of these places exist in the same place at the same time!

And so Henry takes his place on his living boulder. Over time both Henry and the boulder become accustomed to each other and enjoy the way each is able to support the other — the boulder offers comfort and support, and Henry gives the boulder the want to support. The relationship works well.

Gathering her selection of oil paints for this most important event, Ruby prepared herself. The completing of a piece of work is as important, and carries as much weight, as the starting of a painting, the slight difference being to know when to stop as opposed to knowing when to start. Starting, she believes, is when you are feeling good and have the excitement of creativity flowing through your veins. Completing a piece is very much more organic; the work grows to a pinnacle, and it is on that pinnacle that the artist must stop!

Ruby was a master at knowing just when to put her paint brushes back into the waiting jars.

Soft jazz music playing in the background brought Ruby to attention, she stepped back from the canvas and looked very carefully. She could almost hear the movement of the waves, the chattering of rocks and the shoof of seaweed. They were happily interacting. It was then that Ruby saw where she needed to highlight the scene. High in her skyline a shaft of light pushed from behind a silver-white cloud and reached down to the shoreline. She wanted the sky to connect with the shore, so she selected an area of fresh, lime-green, translucent seaweed and chose her final colour. With her palate knife, she picked up a hint of rich, new gold paint, then, very quickly but with delicate care, she made her mark. In that moment the picture was joined together, the Heavens touched the Earth! The jazz playing in the background peaked, and the player went quiet. The painting was complete.

Standing back from her work a silence surrounded the studio, a silence so quiet it was almost deafening, and Ruby began to weep quietly, for, at that moment, she thought about Henry. She knew that there was something not quite right, yet she could not work out what it was. Standing in front of her was a large completed canvas, the canvas was paid for, it was no longer her property but the property of Henry Jones but, the question was,

"Where the hell are you Henry, how will I deliver this to you if I don't know where you are?"

Unaware that she had spoken the last statement quite loud, the emotional build-up of completing her work and the doubts about the whereabouts of her client created a huge outpouring. Ruby stood motionless in front of the canvas and wept uncontrollably.

Finally, she wiped the tears away with the sleeve of her artist's smock and became aware that her studio had suddenly gone darker. She sensed, and then saw, a huge shadow overhead seeming to take forever to pass. Although it had gone darker in the studio the temperature, oddly, stayed the same. Ruby heard a sound that she had not heard for a long time. The singing bowl started softly at first and began to build, deeper resonating tones filling her studio, shadows swooping and diving all around her as she tasted sweet, salty sea mist. Slightly confused but in no way scared, Ruby started to sway with the rhythms of the deep hmmmmmm sound of the song bowls; the breathtaking richness of the sound was filled with joy and happiness. The interior of the studio began to change colour, starting from aquamarine then, below her feet, deepest ultramarine. Ruby felt as if she was suspended in air, but she could hear sounds, and smell and taste aromas. She heard another sound, that of cymbals being played, gently, softly, the sound of metal being struck with felt, the sound building and building a sense of pressure all around her, then the crash of hundreds of cymbals at the same time, trumpet-like shafts of light flashing all around her, images coming in and out of focus. She heard a familiar voice, "I see you made it then, Ruby."

***

Ruby spins around and with an overwhelming feeling of happiness sees, standing in front of her, looking youthful and beaming, Henry Jones!

Ruby says, "But darling, how, how is all of this possible?" His reply is not what she has anticipated. He says, "Never mind all of that, take my hand and let's have fun. After all, you created it!"

Without a thought, Ruby takes Henry's hand and steps into the water which surrounds them, bending, curving, folding. The fish who were dancing to the same tune seem to join fins. Henry begins to laugh as he dances and moves within this watery world. It is infectious. Ruby stretches out her arms and feels the new and invigorating environment that surrounds her. Cymbals crash, song bowls call out with a richness of song that is hauntingly overwhelming. Indian woodwind instruments join in.

Then they enter the deep ultramarine, and again a huge shadow passes overhead. Ruby can see something approaching her from within the big blue. After a second or two, she becomes aware that a gigantic creature is coming towards her. She knows it is a whale and, with its eye focused on her, it comes closer and closer. Ruby knows that she is being invited to touch this most trusting of creatures, for within this eye she understands what is being conveyed — the essence of love and safety in her created realm. Ruby puts out her hand as the whale passes through the invisible cocoon of water in which she and Henry are enveloped. She touches the whale's skin and in that moment rich and overwhelming emotions pass between them. As tears of joy fall from Ruby's face, so they are caught and absorbed into the sea. The whale's eye twinkles as a large diamond-shaped tear falls from its eye onto Ruby's hand. Ruby caresses the tear and puts it to her chest where it is absorbed into her soul. The sound of the singing bowl heightens to a crescendo of rich, colourful sound and all around there is laughter and happy chattering. It is a riot of joy. The whale resumes its gracious dance and soon moves out of sight, its shadow continuing to pass over Ruby accompanied by the singing bowl song.

In changing colour and sound, Ruby finds herself together with Henry travelling into the aquamarine where the sounds of cymbals and drums building tell them that the wave is about to crest and break against the shore. Henry takes Ruby's hand and leads her through the surf up onto the shore. The chattering has become quieter, the mood a little heavier. Henry says, "Dear Ruby we must talk."

Walking along the sand and stones, Ruby looks down and sees that she is barefooted yet she feels no discomfort from the pebbles. Henry says, "Ah yes, no shoes needed here, the only contact is with the canvas, feel the softness. There are no sharp edges here at all. Would you expect anything else?"

Ruby simply smiles and then she says, "But Henry, how is this possible darling?"

Henry looks at Ruby, and he smiles too. "Because you are a wonderful person. You have made it so."

He continues in a calmer tone, "Ruby, even though time has no real influence for me in this, it does for you. You see, I invited you to see future possibilities as I was previously invited."

He tails off quietly then adds, "You will receive by post, a letter from my trusted friend who is a solicitor and his job was to deal with my estate."

Ruby, alarmed, says, "Your estate, what are you saying Henry?"

In a kindly, soft tone, Henry replies, "Oh, Ruby I believe that you know. I believe that deep down you guessed what had taken place?" This is said not as an accusation but as a kind observation.

"Yes Darling, I believe I have known, but I have simply not wished to accept it until now that is."

And then in a happier voice, she says, "But darling! Your visit to me, your telephone call to me, how is that possible?"

Henry, in an upbeat tone, says, "Let's just say that it was. Ruby, it was so exciting to be shown this place, or should I say my happy place, or your happy place, oh, it matters not. The point is that here is a place that when I travelled from your realm into

this realm, I knew I would be happy in forever, and I am!"

Without realising it, Ruby and Henry have walked into a tranquil wooded area where the air is warm but calm and pure. The sound of various percussion instruments playing softly and tin whistle bird song welcomes the artist and her friend. Washboard insect sounds add their song to the ever-growing chorus. Colourful butterfly minims and crotchets flutter all around forming musical scores as they fly together. The silver birches stretch their long branches and bow a deep welcome. Overhead a huge shadow passes by, accompanied by the beautiful, singing bowl song. In this woodland, there is utter tranquillity.

Whilst painting this scene, one of the colours Ruby had selected was zinc white to highlight the light-kissed edges of the slender silver birch trunks. Close up to this paint they could see its components, the paint containing colourful crystals which shimmer and bend the light with the effect of seeming to see the trees breathing, moving as though they were alive. And Ruby can feel them and hear their whispers. She knows them well; after all, silver birches are one of her favourite trees. Other pigments, including copper and silver contained within the colour palette, give a similar effect; the result is an intense feeling of highlighted life and energy.

Under foot, the soft grasses massage the feet of the visitors, and emerald-like gems glint their own welcome as the water droplets fall from the leaves. The crystals contained within the range of pigments refract and reflect light and colour onto every other surface, giving a kaleidoscope effect.

Now, passing through the trees, they are welcomed into a garden, where Hollyhocks, nine feet tall, sway to the music, their plate-sized frilled flowers seeming to smile as Ruby and

Henry pass by. Poppies with paper-thin petals flutter at them as they pass. The range of flowers and trees within the painting is only restricted by imagination and as both Henry and Ruby have differing likes, so the varieties reflect that. The deepest red and purple roses grow next to delicate, old-fashioned sweet peas, their combined aroma sending heads spinning. All of the time music sings forth.

Suddenly, a huge shadow circles in the space above their heads, the singing bowl announces the presence of the whale and other chattering sounds join in. It seems Ruby is somehow creating a euphoric atmosphere and all who dwell within these worlds want to acknowledge their creator.

And so, the ever changing sounds, smells, and scenery continue to alter until Ruby and Henry enter a small clearing surrounded by a host of multi-coloured flowers which greet them with a tiny bow. The grass creates two chair-like mounds for them to sit in.

Henry says, "Shall we continue?"

Ruby replies, in a sweet, childish fashion, "Yes Henry, please do and answer my questions, how and why?"

"The how part is more difficult for me to attempt to answer as I really do not completely understand it myself. Why, is the more straightforward.

"When you pass to the next realm you are given a couple of choices. I chose this realm. As you know I have always loved your work, it has given me many years of enjoyment, and so I made my choice. When asked, where I would like to reside, to me it was simple, to others, it might be very difficult. I will stay here until I am asked again, then I will make another choice. Just like you will be asked at some time in your future and you will have to make a selection."

Ruby seems taken aback at this last remark. Henry sees this on her face and says, "Ruby, Ruby, it is in the nature of things that we have to pass on, to leave where we were born. It is simply part of growing old, the only difference here is that time does not interfere with your life. Even though I have been here since the day you saw me, it feels like only yesterday and, might I add; it feels wonderful. I can recommend it!" He laughs.

This comment soothes Ruby's concerns, and she says quietly, "Yes, I understand, darling, but one does not want to think about dying."

To which Henry replies, "That is the point, Ruby. Having never died before I had no idea what it would be like. In the event which, by the way, was the day I signed the cheque that I left for you, it was seamless, I had ongoing health issues but nothing drastic, then I went to my bed, and that was that."

"Yes, but darling, you called me on the telephone. I answered the door to you; you hung your coat. Are you saying that these events didn't take place?"

"Of course they took place, Ruby, but — and this is the big 'but' — like I said, you are given some choices. I chose to call and visit you; I had been shown how to access paintings because I received a call and a visit from a dear friend who had passed over and was shown the way. Of course, I didn't know that fact when he arrived, but I learned it along the way. That, my dear Ruby, is why I am showing you this."

Henry opens his arms and spreads them indicating all that is around them. As he does so, the sounds seem to applaud gently.

Not completely satisfied with his answer, Ruby asks, "But how did you actually get into the painting when you visited my studio?"

Henry puts his hand into his pocket and produces a small sketch pad and a pencil. He draws a picture frame on the paper; then he sketches the wave. Ruby wonders what he is doing, then Henry takes hold of her hand, places a finger from his other hand into the centre of the pencil sketch, and they both vanish from the silver birch copse.

With a smashing of cymbals and a chattering of voices, Ruby and Henry are once again within a huge wave, once more surrounded by glistening, aquamarine water. Ruby looks at Henry and says, "So that is how you do it, you draw a picture and step in!"

"Yes, in a manner of speaking, you do," Henry replies.

Ruby and Henry begin to laugh loudly, as though just being within the water brings them to hysterics, and, of course, the sea life and music join in.

"Can we stay for another short while? I so want to experience this marvellous place again, darling." Ruby says.

"Yes of course, but then we must finish our talk and you, my dear, must return home."

Cymbals play softly through the wave as the sense of water pressure builds and wraps itself around Ruby. The dance commences, and she is joined by the smaller fish, several octopuses, and tiny, spiny seahorses, flashing with differing colours with every movement. Beneath them in the ultramarine move the gentle giants' shadows, their movements matching the song of the singing bowls and the dance above.

With a smashing of the cymbals, Ruby and Henry walk out from the water and along the shoreline to the waiting boulders where they sit down and look out to sea for several moments, marvelling at the composition and how it looks from within.

In a surprised tone, Ruby says, "The music! In all of the excitement I wasn't really listening to it, but now I hear it, darling, I recognise it. Is it? Could it be?" With tears of joy welling up in her eyes she exclaims, "But of course it is, it is Adam's music, isn't it darling?"

With a broad and understanding smile, Henry Jones nods his head. Ruby says, excitedly, "But how, do tell me, darling, how is this possible?"

Henry sits back into his comfortable boulder and explains, "As much as the painterly and creative process within this work is yours, you share something beautiful with Adam, and that is his music. Don't you see that you are both so creatively entwined that it would not be possible to separate you, and so both your painting and his music are forever captured in the moment, the moment of creativity. It is a joining of talent, a sharing of souls. How wonderful is that my dear Ruby?"

In a quietly reflective voice, Ruby says, "Quite amazingly ace, darling!"

The sun begins to fall in the sky; colours so varied consume the whole of the horizon. Bright red, deep orange, purples, blues, gold and silver, a vast palette of outrageously vibrant colours. It never goes dark in this realm, but beauty must have sunsets. Percussion instruments sound, as yet another colour explodes from within the vista.

It is during the sunset that Ruby becomes aware that Henry has gone silent, not a quiet silence but an out of body silence, and she is not sure how she knows this. Several minutes pass as Ruby continues to enjoy the ever-changing colours. Then she is aware that Henry has arrived back into his body.

Ruby says in an offhand sort of way, "Been somewhere darling?"

Henry looks at her, somewhat amused, and says, "Well, it would appear that you have impressed somebody with some clout. I have been instructed, or perhaps I should say, I have been asked — yes, that's better — I have been asked to continue this tour with you. You are to travel further within this realm. This is truly a gift, a rare gift at that. I must say though, that I am not so surprised.

"But before we continue on our journey I must tell you about the plans I have put in place.

"For me, collecting art has not just been for my personal enjoyment, far from it. I have always known that art within all disciplines gives more to the viewer than simply the item they observe. Art gives much more — hope, happiness, love, and memories. I have been gathering art from many sources, but your work is the highlight of my collection. What I have planned for all of the work I have gathered is a tour of the country, then the world. The collection will be shared with all who need help; those who don't even know they need help, in fact.

"I am not talking about the major galleries. No, it is my intention to make the work available in village halls, community centres, churches, public places — anywhere the general public can see the collection. The events will just happen, there will be no advertising, no grand opening, nothing like that, they will just happen. Some might even happen at the same time as others. You see there are many people who are in need; for them, they will just find the events and visit and they probably will not know why!

"The homeless will be invited to sleep in warmth and will be fed as they are surrounded by the work. All of this is in place, the venues are arranged, all needs will be taken care of. This is just another method of helping those who find it hard to help themselves. Children will attend and will leave, understanding their individual strengths; this, in turn, will support them in their journey forward.

"You see Ruby, we know that all of those who come and look at the work will leave altered in a positive way. And so, where an individual needs comfort, they will receive it; if they are in need of courage, they will have it. And where they need to be loved, they will leave the exhibition knowing love.

"I have worked on these details with the One I visited earlier. It is complicated to explain so just understand that in this realm we can make things a little better than in your realm. Our goal is for all of those who have been assisted in turn to assist others who are also in need."

Ruby remains silent and reflective at the scale of information she has been given. After a time she says, "Darling Henry, what a beautiful and generous notion, and so, how can I assist? I mean I am not here just to enjoy these wonderful displays, am I?"

Henry replies, "You are correct, of course, however, your role in all of this is to carry on with your work. You are in touch with the beauty that resides in life, and you must continue to respond in your way. Simply keep on painting. Your work will continue to be sold, but the network I have put in place will make it possible for all of your work to be present for the exhibition, trust me!"

Ruby exclaims, "Oh but I do darling, I do."

A slight breeze begins to move Ruby's hair. It is warm and sounds like someone gently breathing down a brass instrument to warm up the mouthpiece.

Henry says, "Ah, our time together has come to an end for now. Ruby, you will be taken on your final journey in this realm, enjoy this most spectacular event. I will see you soon."

As Henry completes his words, Ruby finds herself rising into the air, carried by invisible, soft wings. The air surrounding her sings with joy. She can hear below her the sound of the sea washing gently over the pebbles, and she can smell the sweet, sea air as she climbs higher into wispy, white-silver clouds. The clouds caress her and hold her high above the land and sea below. A tin whistle birdsong chorus joins in with the air song, following her brush strokes up the canvas.

Ruby has now left the beautiful scene below, and it seems as though in an instant she is high above the clouds, flying freely without effort on the warm thermals. As she rises, music ascends with her, the air lifting her confidently as a mother would pick up her child. Ruby seems to be able to see forever as if looking into an endless starlit night.

High above she can see a deep ultramarine and purple effect which looks like sky but, within this space, Ruby can see the now familiar deeper coloured shadows moving around, swaying and responding to the ever present song of the singing bowls. She responds with a great, exhilarated sigh and opens her arms wide, wanting to touch as much of this place as possible. She begins to spin slowly, taking in all that is presented to her, the feeling of ultimate freedom all around her. Tin whistling song birds join with her; massive butterflies with wings all the colours of the rainbow, shimmering, floating with the song; smaller musical notes flutter with her, all creating beautiful music.

Then ahead of her, Ruby sees to peaks of majestic mountains and watches as colourful cloud formations speed past the peaks, illuminating them with a wash of refracted light. The chorus continues to build with instruments from all sections of the orchestra joining in, but there is something else present. Ruby cannot see it, but she senses the presence of Another, an entity that is in harmony with all that surrounds her. She feels as though this Entity is, in fact, the Conductor and Ruby knows that the Entity loves her.

The clouds slowly vanish revealing the landscape below, emerald green areas glisten in the light, supporting the mountains which change colour with height. Ribbons of silver and gold wrap around the slopes, sweeping higher and higher until they reach the summit. Then, with the brush strokes that took them there, they continue into the sky, a seamless joining of the land and sky. Flecks of crystal tones shine from all surfaces and rainbow colours reflect each other. The orchestral strings join in, their voices soaring into the ultramarine and purple sky, the double bass sings a duet with the song bowl, the sounds of wind wrap around Ruby and she is completely consumed in the moment.

Passing over the seascapes, the colours change from blue to aquamarine, then turquoise then back to ultramarine. White, silver and golden beaches festooned with every imaginable vibrant pigment interact with the movement of the water and the music.

As Ruby continues on her journey, she suddenly hears the sound of a bell ringing. It is a sound that is so familiar to her! The ringing intensifies but she cannot readily see anything in front of her, so she looks back over her right shoulder. There is nothing but the seascape she has just visited.

✦✦✦

Ruby was standing in front of her easel in her studio. The painting was shimmering as a shaft of sunlight passed through the window and cast an intense ray through the room and onto her canvas. The ringing continued, then Ruby heard Adam's voice clearly talking to a visitor at the front door.

Slightly disoriented, Ruby steadied herself and tried to recall what had just occurred. It seemed that memories that had just been made were dissolving into nothing. She couldn't recall any details of her journey or her meeting, but she did know that something very special had taken place, and then this thought evaporated too, and Ruby remembered what she was about to do.

Casting her ever-critical eye over the now completed canvas, Ruby picked up her signing brush. The signing of a painting is akin to the full stop in an essay; it is the welcome kiss to a friend who has arrived safely following a long journey; it is the soft brush of a hand over the cheek of a new born child. It is the beginning and the end. And so, Ruby selected her favourite, deepest purple paint and confidently signed her work. Then she left the studio to see who was at the door.

***

Deep within the pigments an eruption of sound and movement flashes into life. Singing bowls chorus proclaiming 'joy' together with the sky song. The sea and landscapes rush and join in a beautiful hug. Breaching completely from within the ultramarine, the giant whale beams with ancient contentment. Henry sits on his boulder chair with a look of satisfaction on his face. All around and deep within the realm a rich rejoicing can be heard and felt. The job is complete.

***

Ruby joined Adam who was just entering the inner hall, "Are you OK? You look like you've just seen a ghost!" he asked.

Ruby said nothing. She was looking at the large envelope in Adam's hands. She knew what it contained, but she didn't know how she knew.

Adam said, "It's addressed to both of us — let's have a cuppa and open it."

Ruby made here favourite cup of 'Lady Grey' orange-infused tea; Adam had his 'builders' as he affectionately called the dark liquor. Sitting at the dining table, Ruby carefully inserted the paper knife and with precision opened the letter along the top. When she pulled the opening wide, it revealed several, beautifully hand-written pages of parchment. The letter was headed: *Friends of Henry…*

And Ruby began to read...

My Dearest Ruby and Adam,
By the time you receive my letter, I will have travelled to the next level in my existence, one I know I look forward to very much.

Adam interrupted and said, "What's the date on the letter, Ruby?"

At that moment Ruby recalling some of the details from her recent journey, replied, "Darling, the details are not important, I can explain them later, suffice to say, I know that Henry has passed and that he is indeed very happy."

Adam gave her an odd look, but he knew instinctively to trust her. "Very well, carry on dear."

Ruby read on...

I have given instructions to my trusted friends who will make contact very soon. The travelling exhibition has started, each piece of work that you complete will find its way and join the rest. What I can tell you now is that happiness is being returned to where there was sadness. Light is replacing dark. Music is replacing noise.

We are looking forward to the future that you are both assisting with creating. Keep doing what you do best and who knows we may well meet again in some other place and discuss these matters some more.

Until then.

'Draw yourself a picture and step in,
Fill it with all that makes you happy, not sad,
Make it your special place to escape to,
Keep it safe and close,
It is yours, all that you have drawn is for you,
It will fill your heart.

So go on then, draw yourself a picture,
And step in'

Love from
Henry.

At that moment, Ruby recalled every detail from her visit into the painting, and a wave of deep emotion nearly overwhelmed her. She looked at Adam as he sat with his hands wrapped tightly around his teacup, a tear falling from his eyes as the realisation of what he had just heard filtered through into his mind. Ruby placed a finger softly against his cheek and caught the tears.

"I have lots to tell you, Adam. The details have returned to me, let's go for a walk." Leaving the door open, they took a long walk along the coastline.

***

On a damp and cold late autumn afternoon, a piano accordion played a ghostly melody, a melody that told a story of loss and hardship but, most potently, it told a story of sadness. On a busy street, people could hear the sound, but most did not see where it came from, being too busy with their own lives.

Sitting on her rickety old camping seat was an old woman; who knows, she might not have been so old, but she had endured more than most in her life. Now her only satisfaction was to play the instrument that she loved above all else. Her late father gave the instrument to Sofia when she was seven years old and living on a tiny farmstead with her parents in Europe. Later that year their crops failed, bills were not paid and, to add to their misery, her father passed away from sadness and defeat at not being able to care for his family. So, the time arrived when mother and daughter were forced to move from their land and their home. With her mother and her beloved piano accordion,

Sofia would walk for many miles until they reached some town or village where she would play her beautiful music on streets and walkways, the small amount of cash thrown into her tin mug being just enough to buy food for her mother. Sofia got by on items that had been discarded in bins. After a short period her mother became too sick to continue walking, and so Sofia took her to a church shelter, said her good-byes and left.

Alone in an angry world, Sofia walked through the streets of villages and towns and, as she played her accordion, the music became darker and angry too, but the coins kept trickling into her tin mug. After a cold and particularly wet day, Sofia was able to buy herself a small but adequate meal. As she continued on her solitary journey, she befriended a small group of travelling people who took her in and cared for her, but her sadness remained.

After several years on the road, the travellers arrived in Scotland. The group was somewhat diminished, and Sofia had become one of the breadwinners.

Eventually, she found herself visiting Glasgow, where she would sit for hours playing out her sad story, making just enough to support her adopted family.

She was tired and exhausted. Her tiny wooden-legged seat drew up the damp and cold from the harsh pavements; her thin shoes offered no more warmth. Pedestrians, mostly looking and marching straight ahead, passed her by. Only a handful actually noticed her and listened to the beautifully sad music she played with frozen, sore fingers. There was no longer a smile on Sofia's face — that had faded away years earlier — a look of withered age sat within her weathered, leather-like features, all wrapped up in a woollen head scarf. But still, she played.

It was just as darkness had entered the streets and just before the street lighting appeared that Sofia saw a comforting glow opposite where she was sitting. This glow seemed to beckon her in. She stood up to find that her legs had no feeling, the harsh cold of the pavement squeezing the strength out of her. It took several moments for her to move forward. Still hugging her piano accordion Sofia walked slowly towards the light. Nobody saw her move, neither had anyone noticed the last note she'd played. She was all but invisible to the busy people nursing their own interests.

Reaching the opening, Sofia felt something she had not felt for too long, warmth, not just the warmth from heat but the warmth from love. As Sofia entered, she turned to look at the street where she had spent so many long hours. It was no longer there and in its place was a painting of sea and sky with, in the background, lush, green fields. Sofia thought that she could smell seawater, and then she heard the sound of tin whistles as birds flew through the painting and they seemed to be welcoming her. She placed her now warm fingers onto the accordion keys and joined in with the song that she could hear. She felt the heaviness of her miserable existence evaporate as she played, her music was again beautiful, and it told a different story. It told of happy times with her family.

After a while, Sofia was aware that she was not alone, but she didn't turn around, simply continuing to play with the building chorus of joyful music. A voice at her side said, "Welcome Sofia, I have watched you for some time now, you have helped your friends, and now perhaps it is time for you to be comfortable. Would you like to stay here?"

Without hesitation Sofia said, "Oh yes please, may I?" Sofia's heart wanted to burst with happiness as she knew that her earthly ordeal was at an end.

Henry Jones sketched the scene that was in front of Sofia and told her to place her finger against the sketch.

***

Walking along the soft sandy beach, Sofia sheds her wrinkles and old woollen scarf; her hair shines deep hazel-brown and her eyes sparkle. The smile she had lost so many years ago has returned, and she continues playing her beautiful song, full of happiness and joy. In the distance, she sees two figures she knows at once. She is again with her family.

***

On that Glasgow street nobody realised anything was different, life went on as normal. Not one soul saw the wooden seat vanish into the fabric of the cold, concrete pavement. Inside the wandering exhibition, however, there was great happiness and love.

Travelling from town to town, the exhibition continued on its journey. Sometimes, it could be in several places at one time. Wherever anyone was in need, they would find the exhibition. Some would stay a while and enjoy a cup of tea and the company of the paintings: others needed more and were able to receive what they needed. The exhibition was achieving Henry's dream.

***

Many years have passed in Ruby and Adam's realm, and they have both continued their creative work. As Ruby finished each piece, the sale would take place soon afterwards, a musical score accompanying each one. The system was quite slick. All of the new work would find its way to the travelling exhibition. As Henry would say, 'Where there is a will, there is a way.'

Ruby and Adam spoke at length many times about what they had been allowed to share with Henry, how they were given insight into the Others' realm. As time passed, they both enjoyed several other encounters and heard satisfying updates from Henry. Of course, it was always a great delight and joy to be in the company of all of those who resided in the other realm. On one of these occasions, a new voice could be heard — a musically heartfelt story played on a piano accordion. This music was joined by a whole host of butterfly notes floating gently with the story, enhancing an already stunning performance. The accordion then joined in with the rest of this natural and beautiful orchestra whose music and movement continued to breathe even more life, energy, and laughter all around.

And so, enjoying the passing of the years in their realm and working very hard, both Ruby and Adam looked forward to the time when they could step into their own painting, where they would forever enjoy their special moment together. However, time in this realm does not stand still, in fact, it seems to race by and accelerate with age, but time does not weaken an individual's ability to be creative. On the contrary, the will to get on with the job only strengthens and so Ruby began a new canvas.

This canvas was not on the same scale as many of her other pieces. It was really quite small, but the detail was exquisite. Strong strokes of ultramarine created the feeling of great depth in the sea, this depth gradually changing with a lighter, turquoise green-blue. Then, with added titanium white, the surface was exposed. Shafts of sunlight plunged through the surface of the water, deeper and deeper into the ultramarine and beautiful rays of light touched something in the deep. At a casual glance, there was nothing to be seen, but on closer examination, the shafts of light were being reflected by what looked like a giant, all-knowing eye.

At the first stroke of paint on canvas, the music began. Introduced by the ever-present singing bowl song, the deep bass tone announced the beginning. Indian bamboo riffs joined in, and tiny, tin whistle chords highlighted crystal details. As the chorus built the painting itself started to inhale, its life force so powerful and intense a vibrancy that was pure, surrounded the work. Anticipation floated in the warm air, musical notes hung suspended, waiting.

Standing in front of this painting Ruby and Adam held each other's hand. Ruby said, "Are you, ready darling?"

Adam replied, "Yes, it is time my sweetness, it is the right time!"

Excitedly Ruby exclaimed, "How marvellously ace darling!"

As Ruby sketched the scene containing the sunbeams and the eye, she held it up to the painting. The sound of a singing bowl erupted with a deep resonance; the sound built into a crescendo of cymbals; the painting exploded into vibrant colour and music, and the butterfly notes spun round and round until there was an intense flash of light.

Ruby and Adam were no longer in their former realm, and neither was her last painting.

***

Ruby and Adam walk along the warm, soft, sandy shore, crystals glow all around, and a sense of pure excitement touches them both. Ahead of them, a familiar voice speaks, "Welcome to your new home." Henry Jones is standing in front of them with his arms open wide. Next to him is a shimmering light which reaches out and touches both of them on their faces. Ruby and Adam smile at each other.

***

On an inner city estate, a teenage girl sat on a piece of cardboard under a flight of cold, harsh concrete stairs. Shivering with cold, hungry and unhappy, she was also terribly scared. Life as a runaway was miserable and deep inside she wished she could return to her family. She knew they loved her very dearly, but she felt she had overstepped the mark because of her behaviour and was no longer welcome with them. She had found it difficult to say 'sorry.'

However, the young girl was in need but, like lots of children in her shoes, she was also stubborn and would not ask for help. And so, while she stared out from her windy and cold shelter, she noticed a warm light in the doorway opposite. She hadn't noticed the light previously and it seemed to beckon her.

She decided to investigate. She approached the door and stepped inside.

LOCKED IN

Intense light filled his eyes, pain screamed through his body. John Ross was on his back on a ledge half-way down a fissure in the rocks. He could not focus on anything and lay there in agony for a time. It seemed like hours before his eyes adjusted to the light and he started to see some fuzzy details. Above him was rock — in fact all around him was rock!

"What the fuck is going on?" he said to himself. Then in a flash of clarity he remembered some details. "Holy shit, I fell," he whispered in his mind. "I actually fell," he said to himself in complete disbelief. A shot of pain surged through his entire body making him wince in agony. He lay thinking about the events leading to where he was now.

He remembered leaving the door on the latch at his small croft house, on the Isle of Skye, before collecting his walking boots and ruck sac from the storm porch and placing them in his car. He was about to drive off when he remembered that he had forgotten to leave details of the route of his intended walk for that day.

His wife Alex could not make the adventure as she had to work at short notice, the income was important, so going back inside he left his note:

Glenbrittle, up to Coire Lagan, then back, time now 9'ish, back latest 4'ish, xxxx, John.

Leaving the note on the kitchen table John went back to his

car and, starting the engine, he drove the fifteen miles or so towards Glenbrittle.

A flash of light hit John in his eyes, so intense he wondered how the sunlight was getting to his current location. Then he remembered, that conditions were perfect for walking in the Cuillin — clear blue skies. Continuing his thought process he remembered that, unusually, there was very little traffic on the narrow roads so he'd been able to drive at his pace and take in the outstanding scenery, scenery that he had known for years and yet every time he looked at it, it was like seeing it for the first time. "Wow, comes to mind," John remembered saying out loud. "But I fell, I fell, god damn it!" He said to himself once more. The realisation of his predicament beginning to weigh more heavily on him, "focus," he thought, "focus."

Still attempting to put things together he recalled the excitement building in him as he could see the Cuillin Mountains getting ever closer, he fizzed inside with the magnetic pull of these impressive peaks. He continued his journey around several sweeping bends. On the road sheep stood and looked back at him, not moving, then in their own time trotted to the verge. Buzzards flying high above ascended on the warm air currents, then a golden eagle seemed to hang with ease way above the hills. "The eagle, that's it, I saw the bloody eagle." Another pulse of pain hit him, his breathing became heavy and he rested his mind a while. Several minutes passed and John continued to recount his journey. "Where was I going to?" He thought for a moment, "Glenbrittle, that's it." Now he was following the narrow lane and seeing the Cuillins directly ahead and rising straight out of the sea — dark against the bright blue of the sky, sharp pointed peaks, imposing on the landscape and seen from many miles. "Holly leaves," he said to himself, that's what they're called. And like a magnet they pulled John in.

Another flash of light hit John square in his face; this was accompanied with a jolt of pain. He tried to adjust his position but it was too painful to move. A picture of Alex came to his mind and he started to tremble inside. "Why did she have to work?" He yelled out in frustration.

The track leading to the Fairy Pools on his left, he was almost there. John continued to drive down through this beautiful glen, following the river, then through a farmyard to the open expanse of beach, a natural shallow bay sitting in the shadow of the mountains. Oystercatchers scuttled across the stones and sand as if doing a quick step dance routine, waves gently broke up the sandy beach, a flock of sheep sunbathed on the sand. There were several people walking with family and friends, pitched tents and camper vans. There was also a gentle silence with only the soft sound of the shallow waves breaking then withdrawing from the sand.

He then saw himself parking his car and eagerly donning his boots and grabbing his day rucksack, which was full with the latest climbing gadgets.

"God the pain! And where's that fucking light coming from?" he thought. Wincing again, he was now sweating heavily. "Concentrate, concentrate," he told himself.

Settling slightly, he thought about his next steps getting to where he now lay. Locking his car he had walked parallel with the beach, reached the shower block on the campsite, and stopped to take in the view. He'd breathed deeply. The air was seasoned with the smell of coconut from the rich yellow gorse bushes and it was good.

John began the steep first part of the climb up towards the Coire Lagan. It soon rose to a point where a headland came into view. The sea was several shades of blue, deep ultramarine going into lighter aquamarine. There was not a cloud in the sky and just a light enough breeze to prevent the dreaded midges attacking. A couple of seasoned walkers approached him from ahead. As they got closer they saw John looking at a large house-sized boulder that was just off the track. They stopped and one of them said, "Hi, lovely day, are you on your way up to the ridge? It's so clear today and very few people to get in your way."

John replied, "Not to the ridge today, thought I would take in some of the geology, you know for example, this rock must have been dragged down from the Coire during the last ice age and was left here when the ice retreated!" One of the walkers said, "Yeah, always amazes me what this place shows off. Anyway have a great time, we're off to the Sligachan for an early, liquid lunch. Cheers!" Both men continued down at quite a pace towards the campsite. John thought, "Great, not many people, the place will be all mine." Leaving the large rock with its tree growing out of a crack, he continued to walk up towards the Coire. Soon, though he took another opportunity to take in the views. In the distance he could see the Islands of Rum, Canna, Eigg and Muck. Then he watched a large stag standing quite still. "What does he see?" John said to himself, when suddenly the stag moved and he lost sight of it against the moorland colours. "Brilliant camouflage," he thought. John took a long drink from his water bottle and moved on.

Steadily climbing, John arrived at a point where the path runs through two giant slabs and where he'd had to scramble his way to the top. A little further along still, he was able to look down at a waterfall flowing over the slabs into a deep clear pool making the thought of ditching his clothes and going in for a dip quite inviting. So, as there was nobody in the area, he stripped off and dropped into the clear water for a quick and refreshing dip. John submerged completely into the crystal water and he opened his eyes and could see the marbled effect of the large, smooth pebbles on the bottom. The temperature was good in the shallows as the sun had heated the water as it flowed over the rocks and down a waterfall higher up. Floating on his back looking up into the clear skies every thought and worry washed away; he was so comfortable he wanted to stay longer in the water but felt he had better get out and carry on. He dried off quickly and re-dressed then continued to climb and scramble to the loch. John felt completely invigorated following his spontaneous skinny dip!

The Coire sits at the base of a gigantic amphitheatre, closely surrounded by daunting mountain crags and peaks. The drama of this place was intense and no matter how many times he visited this area he always had a sense that it was for the first time. He sighed a contented breath at the wonder of this place. He found a flat area where he could sit next to the small Loch and decided to have a bit of lunch — an apple, some fruit cake and strong Mull Cheddar. He sat with his back against a small rock and looked around at the spectacular views. He had the warmth of the sun on his face, he listened to the silence and it should have been perfect. Strangely though, he couldn't shake the feeling of guilt of having to leave Alex behind: Alex who needed to earn their keep even on such a perfect day!

After a good rest John thought that the time was right to investigate the unusual sight of a thin vein of basalt that runs through the gabbro. He knew that basalt and gabbro are the same matter formed by a lava flow but that the difference between them is at what speed the lava cools down. To have them running side-by-side, then, alongside deep long gouges in the gabbro, where huge sharp boulders bit into the surface as they were dragged down the mountain during that last ice age are graphic illustrations of the forces of nature that built the Cuillin Mountains. John itched to examine the rocks more closely.

Carefully, he began to walk along the slab of gabbro. It was quite steep, however, but placing the soles of his boots firmly pointing down and leaning slightly back he was able to move down the slab. He could see the vein of basalt just ahead of him on a steeper area and so he carefully edged forward.

"This is it," John said to himself, "the eagle!" Now he remembered exactly what had happened next! He had become aware of a large bird flying just into his line of sight. It was very close. He stopped and looked up to see the large golden eagle just above his head, a wonderful sight. At the same time he looked directly into the full light of the sun which, for a second, blinded his vision. Jerking his head sharply downwards he lost balance. He tried to stay upright but the incline he was on made it impossible for him to retrieve himself. He stumbled forward and fell.

Rolling over and over he hadn't been able to get any purchase, then he was falling through the air. A small gap at the base of the slab had consumed John and he'd collided with an outcrop of rock. He remembered that first agonising, hot pain rush through his body as he came to rest. Disoriented, John tried to look around, he was now absolutely aware that he had fallen and that he was hurt.

Arriving home at about four o'clock, Alex read the brief note from John. She knew he was well trained and even better equipped to go alone into the Cuillin. She thought to herself, slightly amused, "He is quite a gadget king with his g.p.s and other stuff!" However, she was irritated that she had to work. "Pays the bills," she said quietly to herself as she began to make a cup of tea and open the post. She went out and round to the front of the small house. The sun was still high in the sky and, sitting in the warmth with just enough breeze to keep what was left of the midges at bay, Alex enjoyed her cuppa, then thought about supper.

She went to the polytunnel and selected a handful of delicious salad leaves, several ripe, sweet-smelling tomatoes, and a small cucumber. She loved to spend time in the still, warm environment — even when it rained Alex could be found tending to the large variety of home cultivated produce.

She glanced at the clock, it showed five o'clock. Alex thought to herself, "He must have stopped to get a bottle of fizz." She placed the small potatoes in a pan of water and lit the gas ring. When they started to boil, she washed the salad and placed it in a bowl on the plain pine table where fluted glasses rested on place mats. Alex had picked a couple of wild flowers for the table.

Five-forty-five — "Where can he be, this is a little late!" Alex muttered to herself. Six-thirty — Alex went and sat on the door step looking along the lane. There was nothing. She rang his mobile number, never expecting it to be answered, but it did ring and she heard the same message she had heard for years.

"Hi, this is John, I can't take the call at the moment, I must be in the Cuillin having fun, please leave a message or call later." Alex thought that was strange, mad — if he was approaching home there would be no signal at all, the fact that it rang and was connected did not make sense. Six-thirty-five — Alex was beginning to worry about John. She looked at his note — yes, there it stated — *back latest 4 ish.*

Seven o'clock — Alex called the local police station and explained the situation. The officer said he would call the local Mountain Rescue service and ask Neil to call her. In the meantime, he would call the local hospital, just in case.

Seven-twenty — the telephone rang.

"Hi, is this Alex?" A kindly voice asked.

"Yes," replied Alex. "I have been given the full details and wonder if you would be able to drive and meet me in the Glenbrittle car park so that we can look at options — the first is to check if John's car is still there."

Alex turned the oven off and grabbed her car keys. A feeling of emptiness filled her stomach. She drove what seemed a hundred miles; in fact, it was only nineteen. When she arrived, she was met by Neil.

"Can you identify John's car?" asked Neil.

Immediately Alex said in a quiet voice, "Yes, there it is," pointing to a red VW Golf.

Eight-twenty-five — Alex began to fidget. Neil said, "Alex it is important that we speak to everyone in this campsite and anyone who walked out on the route John planned to take. I will do the campsite, you stay next to my van and ask anyone who passes if they have seen John. If you get a positive, call me on this." He handed Alex a small walky-talky and showed her how to use it. Neil then went into the camp site while Alex stood next to the Mountain Rescue van. She was soon joined by another member of the team. "Hi, I'm Steve, you must be Alex," the younger man said, then he spoke into his radio, "This is Neil calling Steve, over."

"Hi Steve, as planned can you do the route and report, please? Over."

"Yes on my way. Out." Steve turned to Alex and said, "As we still have a couple of hours of light left I will do John's route. I can cover the ground very quickly and hopefully report good news very soon."

In a relieved tone Alex said, "Thank you, Steve."

Steve seemed to sprint up into the first hill and was soon out of sight. Alex spoke to several walkers but they could not recall seeing John. She thanked them and they went on their way. She was again joined by Neil who told her, "Well, we have one confirmed sighting of John. He was sitting having some food near the loch. That was around about twelve-ish, so we know he was where he said he was going to be."

Nine-forty-nine.

The shortwave radio crackled; Steve's voice, "Neil, over, come in, Steve."

"Go ahead Steve," Neil replied.

"No trace, I repeat, no trace, I will continue for the next hour or so, then rejoin you, out."

Alex began to tremble at the last message. Neil comforted her and said, "Look, time is slightly against us. Even though it doesn't get really dark, I feel that our best option is to make contact with the rescue volunteers and call them to resume the search from first proper light about. It isn't a cold or wet night so if John is up there the chance that we will locate him in the morning is very good. Conditions are favourable. The best thing for you now is to try get some rest. Now are you OK to drive home or would you like me to drop you off?"

Alex replied, "Thank you but I'll be fine. I'll meet you here at about four, yes?" Neil replied, "Yes, four is fine. We may well have gone up but I'll leave somebody with the control vehicle. Rest well," he added, knowing that Alex would get little if no sleep this night. Steve returned to Neil's location to find Neil calling the Mountain Rescue volunteers.

"Shit! Shit, my rucksack, the g.p.s distress button!" John said to himself. "Move, move yourself." John could see his rucksack to his right-hand side. Forcing himself he stretched out his arm, hot pain shot up into his hand just as he put it onto the soft handle and the jolt made him push the rucksack away. He watched with horror as his 'sack and g.p.s started to slip slowly over the edge. He grabbed for the handle but this made several loose rocks under him move. John began to slide, his body flipped over the edge, the handle fell from his hands, its contents falling faster and hitting something hard below him, then John was in mid-air, falling once more, out of control, then all was darkness.

A light so intense filled his eyes, the light seemed to be swaying from one side to another. John felt no pain, in fact, he felt nothing at all, he fell unconscious again.

John was not aware of how long he had slept when he regained a fuzzy consciousness. He did remember the second fall and could see in slow motion the contents of his rucksack falling out before the blackness. A frightening thought then hit him when he realised that, perhaps he had been where he was for some time, even overnight. That thought created an overwhelming surge of emotion within his mind and he called, "Alex, Alex where are you? I need you!" He wanted to cry but nothing happened, no tears, just the painful emotion of dread and fear. And still no pain.

Two in the morning on the following day Alex was sitting in her car at the Glenbrittle car park. She had not slept, and so she'd driven to the beauty spot to wait for Neil and his team. She felt as though she had just dropped off when she heard the sound of several vehicles parking up, then the sound of voices.

She quickly got out of her car and spotted Neil. She waved. Neil walked across to her and indicated for the fourteen other mountain rescuers to meet her. Alex immediately thanked the team for their efforts. Getting his maps set out on the bonnet of the control car Neil briefed the team.

"We can place John next to the Loch, he ate there, that is the only piece of information we have. We also know that the time was about midday — assuming he intended to return home for about four in the afternoon, that would have given him a maximum of two hours to look around, so we can rule out the Ridge. John had an interest in geology and enjoyed looking at the gabbro areas, so that must be our starting point. Three teams, one on top of the gabbro slab, the other running parallel at its base and one will take the route up from the Youth Hostel, just in case John went that way. Are we ready, any questions?"

Alex said, "Would it be OK if I came with you, I am mountain fit, please may I come?"

Neil replied in a firm but gentle tone, "Alex, I understand that you very much want to assist. However, you would get in our way. We have a search method — that is why we are leaving so early, that is why for the time being no one will be allowed into the area so, with regret, you must remain here. You can continue to ask visitors if they saw John yesterday. We will be in contact with Andrew who is the control. Please give us the time we need to do our best." The teams completed a radio check then team three headed for the youth hostel while the other two teams left at a swift pace into the Cuillin.

The interior of the space that John was in began to cast shadows. He realised that the sun was getting higher. He attempted to move his arms, nothing. His left then right leg, nothing. He thought about his breathing, "Well I still have function so not all is bad, but why no pain nor movement in my limbs?" It was following this thought that a possible reality slammed into John's mind: "Oh God, I'm paralysed, that must be the only answer. Oh God, they will never find me!" The reality of this one thought blinded John of all other thoughts. His mind reeled, he screamed but no sound left his lips, he cried but no tears fell from his eyes. Then for a second John thought that he heard something, muffled at first, but then clearer. It was a call, quiet at first then louder. John could hear the words being called.

"John, John, if you can hear us call out." Then he heard the call again but coming from somewhere much closer. In his mind, John was screaming at the top of his voice, but nothing escaped his lips.

"Here, here, I'm down here!" John called within his mind, again and again, but there was still no sound.

Then John saw shadows moving in the light right above him, and the sound of the call was much louder. He saw what looked like a shaft of concentrated light, probably from a powerful torch. "I am here; please hear me, I am below you, Oh God, please hear me!"

Standing above the gully into which John had fallen, one of the search team looked into the steep sided hole. Shining his touch into the deep vertical sides, he saw only what appeared to be the bottom of this shallow gully. He could not see where the edge of the next ledge and the deeper drop off started as they blended into one solid-looking mass of rock.

In the car park, Andrew waited for any information; then there was a crackle. Alex, who was standing outside of the vehicle, took a sharp intake of breath as she heard the radio noise. She listened as the first message came through.

"Control, control, this is Neil over, come in, over."

Andrew pressed the receiver button and said, "Control, this is Andrew go ahead Neil, over." The reply came. Alex held her breath, her chest felt a crushing sensation, and her hands were trembling.

"Negative result so far, please call for the dog search unit, they should have reached Skye by now. Inform them to come straight to the scene, over."

Andrew replied, "Message received, calling dogs now, out."

Andrew picked up another radio telephone transmitter and put in the call. Alex stood frozen to the spot, quietly weeping.

The calling John had heard became fainter. However, he continued to scream from within. He was exhausted with the mental effort and for several minutes, or was it hours, he fell still again. His eyes watched as the shadows moved slowly around the only spot of reference he could see. He had no power of movement in his eyes, he had no movement apart from the involuntary rise and fall of his chest cavity as his body automatically inhaled shallow breaths of air. Staring at the slowly moving shadows, John became aware of a different sound. All of a sudden into his field of vision came a huge shining nose, then a huge tongue appeared and John heard a single loud bark of a dog. The dog barked again and again but did not move. John felt a feeling of euphoria envelope his mind. "They've found me, I'm safe," he cried to himself.

At the control vehicle, the radio crackled. Andrew picked up the handset. Alex, who was sitting on the grass verge next to the van, looked up. Hope was draining away from her.

"Control from search one, come in, over." The tone sounded different to the previous message. Andrew replied, "Go ahead Neil, over."

"Contact Air Sea Rescue a.s.a.p, we have located the casualty, need immediate evacuation, over!"

"Will do, out." Andrew immediately picked up the other handset and placed the call.

Alex jumped to her feet, hope returned. Excitement rushed through her body; tears of joy ran freely down her face. She leaned into the vehicle and kissed Andrew. He blushed but said nothing. Alex said, "Thank you, thank you."

Andrew called Neil.

"Control to search one, over."

"Yes go ahead, over."

"Air support unit airborne, e.t.a twenty minutes, over."

"Yes, received over." Then Andrew said, "Control to search one over, ten six, over?" Alex knew this was a code which asked the casualty's condition.

Neil replied, "Almost ten, ten, over."

Andrew looked at Alex and said, "Alex, things are not looking good up there. They have located John, but the search doctor has said he's in a bad way, the Air Sea Rescue will be here very soon and will evacuate him to Queen Elizabeth spinal unit in Glasgow."

As Andrew finished talking, in the distance but out of sight, the sound of rotor blades could be heard, then after a few more minutes, Alex saw the lights from the red and white air rescue helicopter. Alex watched helplessly as the helicopter flew in from a southerly direction on the west side of the Cuillin Ridge. Even from this distance, the sound of the rotor blades were loud. The aircraft banked to its left and disappeared into the natural crater of the Coire Lagan.

After what seemed to take an hour or so, the radio crackled again. "Control from search one, over." "Yes, go ahead Neil, over," Andrew responded.

"Search doctor has suggested that we collect patient's wife and take to Glasgow over, prepare Alex, over."

Andrew replied, "Will do! Out."

Andrew called Alex to the vehicle. She had been glued to the spot watching for movement from the helicopter. He said, "Alex, they would like you to travel to Glasgow with John, so get your things from the car and get ready, they're about to leave."

Alex in shock said, "What about the cars?" Andrew replied, "Just leave the keys with me, and we will sort things out."

The roar of the helicopter engines got louder as it approached the large field adjacent to the campsite. It landed, and Andrew led Alex to the opened aircraft door. The crew assisted her inside where she was secured into a seat. The huge engine rattled as they lifted off heading out of the Cuillins. Inside the aircraft, the onboard doctor, Steve Morden, spoke to Alex.

"Alex, can you hear me?" Alex nodded.

"Alex, John has had a bad fall. He is alive, however his vital signs are weak. I want you to move to where I am and speak to John. I believe that he will hear you. You will have to be strong Alex, are you up to it?" Alex nodded. She moved closer to where she could see her husband cocooned in silver quilted insulating sheets. His head was strapped into a thick neck brace, a set of earphones over his ears. Alex looked at her husband and took a sharp intake of breath when she saw that his eyes were wide open. They stared forward. His face was the same as the last time she had seen him. Alex lightly kissed John on the lips and whispered, "Oh John, I love you, I can't lose you John, stay with me!" Hot tears flowed down her face. She looked directly into his eyes — there was no response.

Following the barking sounds, John had heard shouting but could see nothing. He thought, "I'm saved, they've got to me, thank God, thank God." Then, he'd passed out once more. The next voice he heard was Alex. He was looking directly into her eyes, his mind raced, and he called out, "Alex, Alex thank God, I love you, thank God." Alex heard no words as he again lost consciousness. His eyes, however, remained open. John would remain unconscious for the next thirty five days.

To John the image he focused on was white. He had no concept of time, or where he was, he could not hear anything apart from the regular ping of machinery. Then a bright light was shone straight into his eyes, and a voice said, "We saw the monitor spike fall, so we called you, doctor."

John shouted, "I'm awake, help me, look at me, test me, I am awake! Please help me; I'm awake." His inner words tailed off and John inwardly wept.

The doctor replied, "Well there is no evidence of change, keep monitoring," then he said, "Strange, his eyes seem to be seeing, but with no other evidence it is difficult to say if there is any brain function at all!" John heard the sound of a door swish then all was quiet. The lights were dimmed, and again there was silence apart from the rhythmic pings.

Over time visits became routine. Alex would appear in John's line of sight; she would tell him she loved him and wished that there was something more she could do for him.

John would continue to shout, "I'm here, I'm here! Just look closer, I am here!" But to no response.

On a regular basis, a blinding light would be shone into his eyes, and the same comment made, "No change."

Four months had passed, and it occurred to John that to him it seemed as if time did not exist, that things simply appeared in his line of sight. There were a few one-way conversations then dim light then lighter light, but he did not sense time.

It was following a visit from Alex that John continued to shout as Alex had become overwhelmed with sadness and John caught the sight of tears in her eyes. John continued to shout for what seemed like hours.

While in the middle of another screaming and shouting bout John heard another voice. He had not heard the usual swish of the door, and this voice was different. Then he heard, "OK John, that is enough of the noise, you are deafening us!"

John was silent, and he thought "Who was that?"

"That, that was me. I have been tracking you down for weeks, the noise you have been making definitely got our attention, John!"

The reply was said in a sort of humorous tone.

"Yes, John you have certainly got a set of bellows."

John remained silent, waiting for an image to cross his vision but nothing came.

He quietly asked, "You can hear me, you can actually hear me?"

"Yes," came the kindly reply. "John, I'm not in the room, I'm communicating directly to your mind."

John said, "But how?"

The voice in John's mind became more serious and said, "John, you are trapped between your physical life, that is your body, and another dimension where I and others dwell. We call it being 'locked in'."

"What do you mean locked in another dimension, what are you, an Angel or something?"

The voice calmly said, "No John I am not an Angel. They dwell in another dimension; this dimension is en route to that other dimension."

John broke in, "Stop right there. What are you talking about, other dimensions? Is this some sort of dream I'm in, am I going mad, will I wake up any second?"

The reply silenced John.

"No John, the truth is that you have been involved in a catastrophic accident, the doctors believe that you are all but brain dead and you are being kept alive by a machine. What they do not know is that there is a part of you that is very much alive and you exhibited that on one occasion a while ago, and so they wait for another sign. It is however only a matter of time before the technology keeping you in this realm will be switched off, and so I am here to guide you, John."

Taken aback by the bluntness of the statement John said, "But what can I do about anything, I am useless!"

"John, John, the reason I am here is because you are not useless at all. You have managed to cross from this realm into another, you have exhibited great strength of mind in doing so. That is why we could hear your noise, and that was how we were able to track you here. No, far from it, you are strong, and that strength will assist you in whichever route you choose to take."

John said in a surprised and incredulous tone, "Are you telling me that I have choices? Like I can get up and resume my previous life, just walk straight out of here!"

The visitor said, "No John, sadly the choices you have are very different. If you choose to stay in this realm, you will remain in your present situation. Some people prefer that, they accept that what they have, I mean the love from their family, is sufficient. They are content to fade in their own time. Others give themselves freely and make the small but significant step to the next dimension. John, you are quite different, your strength is untested, we have no idea of what you might be able to achieve, what we do know is that we heard you, and we were able to follow your noise."

John responded, "So how are we communicating now, is it some sort of psychic stuff?"

"No, look you are wired up, all sorts of probes are attached to you, mainly to your brain. These are linked into a main computer. Every computer is linked together; you can find where they join. So when we heard you calling we simply followed your signal, then when you lost consciousness we lost your signal. Your latest noise was so loud, and so long we were able to find you very quickly."

Still confused, John said, "And so how can you hear noise if you're in another realm?"

"All realms are linked together. However, unless you look and see, you cannot detect where they link. If you do not listen and hear, then you cannot hear where they link. It is quite simple John; the human brain was designed to do so much more. Sadly the way you evolved meant that you pushed aside your brain power in preference to your brawn power.

There are and have always been those who could and did use more of their capacity, mostly they were shunned, not believed, called witches and fools. But they could see, and they listened well. Take a look at the Native Americans for example; the Inuit have seen and listened since they were born. And so, John, the waves of information passing through space also pass through the other realms. Think of it like a transistor radio on the widest band."

John replied, "And so you're telling me that I have somehow

accessed my higher brain function and am able to find my way around all of the avenues you have told me about?"

"Yes in a roundabout way, John, well said."

"So can you tell me what the next dimension or realm is, where it is, and by the way, do you have a name?"

"Oh, yes how silly of me, my name in its simplest form is Emanuel, and all realms exist together, so are you on for the ride?"

John said in a quiet tone, "I suppose I have nothing to lose."

Emanuel said, "Hop on board then." There was something familiar about Emanuel's voice.

Alex and John had been married for ten years. They met while working together in Cumbria. Alex worked for a firm of accountants; her portfolio contained the small chain of restaurants that John managed.

The wedding followed a perfect, whirlwind romance, a quiet ceremony with close friends and family. The music played for them was *A Lover's Concerto,* which completed the day when they committed to each other for life. They were both lovers and best friends.

John and Alex loved the outdoor life style, and so made the decision to grasp the nettle and relocate from Cumbria to the beautiful Isle of Skye. Alex continued to work for a local accountancy firm, but on a part-time basis, John advertised himself as a 'Handyman'. His work kept him mobile and in the outdoors. The best part of this deal was that they both had flexibility — less income of course, but they enjoyed their new life styles. Both enjoyed walking, kayaking, cross-country skiing in the winter, and loved to explore the wonderful and diverse Highlands and Islands.

Alex tried to contain her emotions following the accident. Her life was turned inside out, a nomad, travelling between Skye to Glasgow, always hopeful that good news was just around the corner. Sadly such news was always just out of reach, so Alex trudged on. She was offered help from the spinal unit support centre. Gentle counselling seemed to release some of the grief she was enduring. It was suggested that she compose letters for John, expressing her feelings for him and her own feelings. In this way at least she was not bottling up her emotions.

Following her latest visit, Alex returned to their home and thought about how she would begin her first letter to John. She made herself a cup of tea then listened to the many recorded messages that had been left on the answer unit. Most of the callers simply wanted to offer heartfelt support and love to both Alex and John, a couple were invitations for dinner and so on.

Alex sat at the dining table and picked up her pen. The pen hovered over the note pad in front of her. She would begin with, 'My Dearest John, God how I miss you,' then tears would begin to flow, and the paper would join the rest of the many scrunched up sheets in the large wicker basket next to the table. This is just no good, Alex thought to herself. It seemed that the very action of writing down on paper was too difficult, too intimate, too hard.

Alex sat back; she heard a message being delivered on her laptop. 'Ping ping' was her chosen audible alarm. This made Alex think that it might be easier to use the keyboard to write rather than the physicality of using a pen. Placing the keyboard on the table, Alex began to tap.

As this note was akin to sending an email, there was no formality. She started,

Hi John, just got back home, happy to be sitting having a cuppa.

This approach seemed to work for Alex. She continued,

Had a call from Jan and Jim today, they send their love and will visit in a week or so. Work has been so supportive with the work load; I must get to the office as my desk is getting cluttered. Oh, John, I miss you so much. I will wait for you.

The typing stopped as tears flowed once again down her face. Leaving the table she went for a walk, returning twenty-five minutes later. Feeling much better about things she sat at the table and touched the laptop screen which immediately flickered into life. She read what she had written, then said to herself, "did I write that?" Typed at the end of the note was,

I love you.

She smiled.

It seemed to John that he was travelling at high speed along a brightly coloured tunnel, flashing lights all around, junctions peeling off, taking him down more lit tunnels. Then John came to a stop. His guide Emanuel said, "I brought you here because I want you to see into the other realm. There is a portal just over there where you can see more clearly." John saw what looked like an observation platform against the side of the tunnel.

It suddenly occurred to him that he could hear Emanuel but not see him. John said, "Emanuel where are you, I can hear you but where are you?"

Emanuel replied, "I am within our realm, I cannot cross over to yours. However, I can communicate with you. Likewise, you cannot enter our realm because you still reside in your realm, but we can communicate."

What was it about Emanuel that was so familiar to John? He put the thought to one side before stepping onto the platform. In front of him was a gap in the structure. At first, it was unclear what John was looking into as there was no real detail. Then as though travelling towards him at great speed details began to emerge. John could see into a room. In the room was a table; sitting on the table was a mug and a laptop computer. John immediately recognised this room; it was his kitchen at his home. In an excited tone, John said: "But how?" Emanuel answered, "All of the realms coexist, John. They are linked in a sort of loop. I suppose you could say they would appear like the circles on the Olympic flag. All of the realms have common factors, and therefore we can communicate." John said, "So why can't we see into other realms?"

"You can, John, but like I have said you choose not to."

Emanuel continued, "If you look at matters in this way: you

were born into the third dimension, you grew up, and you learned. However, your brain is capable of so much more. Some people have used more of their brains and prevented millions of deaths, while sadly others have used their brains and have been responsible for millions of deaths. But on the whole what you use in your dimension is so little — but it is enough to prepare you for entering this realm. And so, perhaps you should see your dimension as a training ground for the next, and so it goes on until you reach the ultimate realm. I do not know what happens then, but I have a good feeling about it."

John looked into the portal and saw Alex entering the room. In an instant, John said, "I love you."

"No!" exclaimed Emanuel. It was too late — Alex sat at her table and saw the three words at the end of her text.

"We must move on; I would like to show you more as time is now precious."

John stepped off the lookout point and was whisked away along the light tubes. He asked, "Why did you say 'no' back there, was it wrong?"

Emanuel answered, "There is one thing that binds all of the realms together. It is called many different names, but you will understand the word 'Love'. It is a word that when truly meant can cross many boundaries, it is the purest of all, it is invisible, but it holds the key to everything. You, that is to say, you and Alex, have such a strong love it bonds you together, and so when you said 'I love you', the strength of feeling and love within you sent that message, and it entered the laptop where it appeared as text."

John said, "So can I send messages when I want?"

Emanuel said, "Do you really think it would be helpful, or would it simply confuse matters? That is what you must determine!"

As they continued their progress through the tunnels, John could see what he thought were stars and planets. They were just visible through the light. Colours of all different kinds whisked passed them. John said, "What am I seeing through the light? They look like stars."

Emanuel replied, "They are stars, John. Even though the other realms are linked, the rings in which they travel pass through time and space. You see, all time and space are linked. Entering the different realms with knowledge and understanding gathered allows you to travel through the rings and to see other dimensions. But whether you can enter those dimensions is not clear to me yet, perhaps in another time I will understand the answer."

John said, "Does time travel at the same speed in your dimension as in the others?"

Emanuel replied, "It would seem that time passes at a different rate depending on which realm you dwell in. Time in your realm would seem to pass quickly when you are older but much more slowly when you are younger. Time is also about how we feel about things. And then, even as time travels by we can stand still: just like travelling on a tube train, you get off at the next station and wait."

John said, "How is time affecting you?"

This question seemed to take Emanuel by surprise, then he said, "I am on a platform waiting for a train to arrive." The tone was slightly saddened.

John then said, "Can you travel this way in my dimension?"

"No John, when you are born you begin a journey. This journey is greatly dependant on the choices you make. Sometimes those choices are made for you, but mostly you make them for yourself. For example, you can choose to be kind, or you can choose to be unkind, to love and receive love or indeed dismiss love — the choices are yours to make.

"What you cannot make a choice in is whether you die or not. In your realm it is inevitable that you will die: you cannot slow down time as you can in other realms, but as I have said when you pass to the next realm you take with you what you have learned. Of course, some take with them negative notions; for those, time stands still until they think and come to, let's say, a more acceptable way forward. John, you have been given a gift, you have seen what most never see until they pass over. Embrace it, John."

Continuing the progress, John asked, "We seem to be travelling in one direction! Can we travel in the opposite direction?"

Emanuel said, "Yes, of course, we can. However, travelling in the other direction will take you back into your history, you would see where you have travelled through your life. I suppose it would not harm to walk down memory lane would it?" This was said with a hint of humour.

Turning about John saw an opening in the other direction. "That wasn't there a second ago!" he said in surprise.

Emanuel replied, "You see John, the journey we are taking is your journey. You might have noticed that we have not met any other being while we have been travelling. It is because this is your space, you cannot enter any other being's space and neither can they enter yours. Ahh, here we are."

In front of John was another viewing platform. He stepped onto it and saw familiar scenery. Spreading out in front of him was his junior school playing field. The field was packed with children, mothers, and fathers. The parents were standing at the far end and either side of a roped-off, straight length of grass. Teachers held a thin tape which kept the ten youngsters in a line, then a whistle sounded. The tape was dropped, and the young boys ran forward.

John recognised himself in the middle of the group. His child self had determination on his face as he pumped his little arms and ran as quickly as he could. John junior pushed himself and reached the end ribbon in first place, a look of joy on his small face. The scene changed, and John recognised himself, probably at the age of fourteen, once again on a playing field. This time a game of rugby was taking place. The ball was kicked up high then fell quickly towards the ground — waiting to receive the ball was John. Catching the ball, he ran with astonishing speed.

The opposition began to home in on him, the try line was a short distance ahead, he could do it, and then as the opposition took their position to tackle him, he launched the ball to a team mate ten metres to his left. It flew and landed into the waiting arms of his team mate who crossed the try line to great applause.

Emanuel said, "Great pass John. However, the reason for showing you this game is to demonstrate how you have conducted your life. Even with the try line directly in front of you, you were willing to pass the ball to another. You made the right choice."

The scene changed again. This time John was in his twenties. He was in smart clothes and was sitting at a restaurant table. Sitting opposite him, in the light of a candle, was Alex. Her face was serene, she was smiling and looking directly into John's eyes. He was holding her hands across the table then Alex said softly, "I love you, John, I am so happy to become Mrs. Alex Ross tomorrow, I want to be with you forever."

John felt a wave of emotion wash over him as the scene evaporated. He stepped off the view point and, turning back to the original direction; John continued along the tunnel.

Then, in front of John appeared a flash of intense light and everything appeared to stop, there was an intense blackness immediately followed by clinical white light and John could hear different voices. The voices were excited: "Call Dr. Spink, the monitor has gone crazy!" John was staring straight up when he heard a familiar swish as the door opened and footsteps approached. A bright light entered his field of vision as Dr. Spink scanned his inner eyes and said, "Strange, still no optical response. Did you calibrate the monitors? That is a huge electrical spike!"

In a panic, John called out, "Emanuel, what's happening?"

Calmly replying Emanuel said, "John our time is even more precious than I first believed, we must continue!"

John said, "But what happened then, the light, the dark?"

Emanuel replied, "You are very much alive in your dimension, and the electrical energy that you are using to navigate these realms has begun to activate the sensors to which you are attached. For the time this activity is not understood by those who are caring for you, but they will make more in-depth examinations and discover that you are not simply 'locked in', so come, let us continue."

Without argument, John followed the guide's voice. They travelled through the stars and then took a slightly different coloured route. This tunnel was made of pure white light. As soon as John entered this light, he felt a serene calmness caress him. He felt as though he wanted to weep with happiness and joy.

John arrived at another portal. Stepping onto the platform, he could see what looked like a meadow. However, the meadow was not green in colour but iridescent shimmering silver and white pure bright light.

John said, "What is this place?"

Emanuel said, "This place John, is where you ascend into pure peace. From here I believe you go to your final destination. I will in time reach this place, but first I have many matters to attend to."

John said, "Why do I have this feeling of pure happiness within me. Why do I want to cry with joy?"

Emanuel said, "This realm cleanses you, your energy becomes pure, you become at one with everything, and then you are accepted beyond. What you sense, even from this distance, is 'love'. Like I have said, love is the most powerful force in all of existence. Come now, we have one more place to visit."

Stepping off the viewpoint and returning into the series of tunnels, John was again travelling. Suddenly he was out of the beautiful white light and back into the coloured tunnels of light. Again it seemed as if he was travelling at immense speed.

Suddenly, as before, John was aware of a blinding white light followed by a blackness, and then in his line of sight, he was in the other place. This time it was different. John was aware of lots of activity around him, voices talking, shadows dancing in grey tones on the ceiling within his line of vision. The voices were talking in an excited tone; then he heard a familiar voice: "Yes, Thomas I saw that, incredible, it would seem that the electrical pulses are indeed sparking responses within his higher brain function. We must maintain a constant observation, I must think about the possibilities, never before I have seen such activity!"

John said, "Are you there Emanuel?"

"I am John, I am indeed. I have never left."

John said, "What does this mean, help me understand!"

Emanuel replied, "There is no time for explanations John, we need to visit one last location."

"Where?" John asked, slightly confused.

Emanuel said, "Just follow."

Once again John found himself travelling through the brightly coloured tunnels. This time his journey seemed to take more effort, almost as if he was travelling through treacle. Each movement demanded more effort, the lights slowed down but soon he arrived at a familiar junction. Instinctively he knew which branch to take and soon he was at the platform that gave a view into the familiar kitchen space with the table and hot mug of tea.

Sitting at the table was Alex. She sipped from her cup then placed it on the table in front of her. The screen of her laptop was erect, and she was typing on the keyboard.

John watched.

Alex began to type a note:

My dearest John, we have done so many wonderful things together, adventures, excitement, but most of all we have enjoyed each other. You are so much a part of my whole self, and I am part of yours. The promises we made to each other in front of our friends, family, and God, still hold now as strongly as the day we made them. John, I have loved you with all of my heart and will forever do so. I will wait for you until the time we are once again reunited.

Our love for each other is a potent thing. It will sustain us, I now know and understand that, like a great big yellow balloon that takes flight from your hands, and as the balloon rises and slowly disappears from your view, the balloon does not reduce in size, it only reduces in your vision. In fact, the balloon remains the same size and when it disappears from your view, it appears and grows in size in another space. It is still a large yellow balloon. I love you with all of my heart, my dearest John. Alex.

Closing the laptop down, she sat back in her chair and once again smiled to herself. She picked up her mug of tea and drank deeply from it. As if watching this episode unfold from the outside of a glass bowl, John was suddenly reminded about the situation in which he found himself. He felt the pure emotion that had just been expressed by his wife but held back the urge to force a response as he recalled Emanuel's words. Invisible tears welled up within him, and he cried.

There was a comforting silence exuded from Emanuel, then he said to John, "Our time is completed, the strength you have exhibited is building, and the path you need to take has presented itself. You must know John that it has been my pleasure to be your guide. Who knows that in some other time and realm we might even discuss this encounter. On the other hand, we may not. Some matters are yet to be resolved. Just know John that 'love' is, and has always been, the answer, sleep well."

In a side ward at a hospital, John Ross was surrounded by staff. The room was filled with monitors, bleeping sounds, the swish of the door constantly opening and closing. There was an excitement; John could sense it. Then a familiar voice spoke, "I've seen the monitor displays and had them analysed. We seem to be getting him back; the spikes are off the scale and yet

I can't detect any physical signs. Perhaps we can try stimulation, let's start with temperature."

John was quite calm; he was mulling over what he had encountered. "Was it real?" he mused, "It must have been — the detail, the emotion, how could it not have been real? But what is going on now, where do I go from now? Alex will be here soon, just to see her face."

John's thoughts were suddenly halted as he felt a sharp stab of cold, followed by a burst of intense heat, he winced. Dr. Spink watched as John's right hand was immersed into a bowl containing iced water. The hand was left there for several seconds then removed and plunged into hot water. This generated an immediate reaction as John's whole body twitched.

Dr. Spink said, "I knew it, I knew it, his neural electrical senses are reconnecting." Then Dr. Spink said, "John I'm sure you can hear me, you must concentrate, focus on a part of your body and call us! Move any part of your body, any; I have faith in you, John, just do it!"

There was real emotion coming from Dr. Spink. He had taken personal charge of John and had grown to like his patient. Not quite understanding what was taking place, he knew that the mind was indeed a complex organ with the capability to surprise even the most eminent of doctors.

"I can do this, I can do this," John said to himself. Focusing his mind, he began to visualise his nerve pathways. He could see his fingertips and how they were linked to his mind. He followed the track of his nerves and, when he had the full picture in his mind, to himself he shouted, "Now!" As he sent a thought from his mind down along his spinal cord, then branching off down his right arm into his fingers, he felt the electrical pulse surge through his arm. It smashed into his wrist then spread into his fingers, crashing into his fingertips.

Watching for any sign, Dr. Spink waited. He was holding his breath when in an instant John's right hand convulsed and flexed. In an excited voice Dr. Spink said, "Again John, again my boy, we are waiting for you!"

From deep within his brain John concentrated all of his efforts. He could feel sensations rushing through his body, the flood gates had been opened and electrical pulses began to pour out, travelling at high speed throughout him. With even more effort John forced his mind. The energy built up, he held his concentration then let it go.

Around the bed everyone waited for a response, the anticipation was high. They had all cared for John. After what seemed like long minutes the tension in the room abated. A feeling of 'in time' travelled through the staff. The door was opened with the usual swish.

John could feel the intensity of electrical pulses building inside of him. From almost a standing start sparks began to occur, travelling along his spinal cord. As the surge built, John felt his whole body jerk into life. Again and again, surges and pulses pumped life back into dormant tissue.

As the door swished open and several of the staff started to leave, they heard John's breathing become stronger. They re-entered the room and with wide eyes watched as John's body began to flinch. Then there was a jerk followed by an exploding shout from John, "Yes!" The words shocked everyone in the room, some of the staff quietly cried tears of joy. Then John shouted again, "Yes, yes!"

Following the extraordinary events of the previous day, John had fallen into a deep sleep. He was now only attached to a couple of brain monitors. His breathing was stable, and his brain function was normal.

Waking up several hours later, John opened his eyes. His first sight was Dr. Spink who had spent the whole night sitting next to John, watching and waiting. He had many question for John, but they would wait.

John shifted position in his bed and quietly said: "Where am I?"

In a gentle, fatherly tone Dr. Spink said, "John, my dear boy, you are safe. You are in hospital following a serious accident; we can talk later, now you must rest."

John said, "But I can move — I thought I was paralysed!"

Dr. Spink gave him an odd look: "Why would you say that John, you have been in a coma for several weeks, but your body is fine as far as we are concerned!"

John said, "Where is Alex, have you called her? She'll be waiting for a call."

Dr. Spink considered the request for a while then said, "John, you were involved in a serious road traffic accident."

John said, "But I fell, lost my balance on the Coire Lagan. I could see and hear everything; it wasn't a car accident!"

Dr. Spink said, "No John, you were involved in a road traffic accident. You were travelling on the M6 motorway; there was a thick fog bank. There was no warning. It was a multi-vehicle collision. As far as I am aware you were en route to the Highlands the Isle of Skye I understand, for a walking holiday with Alex."

John interrupted, "This is wrong, I had just gone for a walk. Alex couldn't make it; she had to work, this is all wrong!"

Dr Spink leaned closer to John and gently said, "John, listen to me carefully, you were travelling in your car with Alex when you were involved in a terrible road traffic accident. Many people did not survive this terrible tragedy."

John interrupted again, "Alex, where is Alex, have you called her? I left her a note; she'll be worried!" There was tense confusion in John's voice.

Dr. Spink said, "John, there were many casualties that day, many people were killed. John, I am so terribly sorry to say that Alex did not make it. She didn't suffer; she died instantly." He paused then continued, "You have been here for several months, John. You received minor injuries but had a serious concussion. You then fell into a deep coma. We thought you would not make it!"

Not hearing the last part of the statement, John said, "But we live on Skye, Alex couldn't join me on the walk, she had to work. I left her a note; I told her I would be back at four!" Then he lowered his head and quietly said, "Then I saw her sitting at the table, and she wrote to me. Oh God, what is happening?"

Dr. Spink replied, "It would seem reasonable to surmise that as you were heading to the Highlands, you had talked about what you might do, or your aspirations, your vision of a possible future living together on Skye. And so when the accident happened, you may well have been discussing just that! When you arrived here, you dived into a deep coma. It is true, we as doctors know little about what goes on in the depths of a human mind. What we do know is that the human mind creates its own versions of events. Reported accounts suggest that a person can live a happy and complete life while in a deep dream state. This would appear to be what you have experienced. It would seem appropriate for you to hold onto the happy memories you enjoyed with Alex."

Within two weeks John made a full recovery. He had many conversation with Dr. Spink, and he became a close and welcomed friend. John left the Cumbrian hospital and returned to his family home in a small village. The news he had received hit John very hard. He could barely accept that his loving wife was no longer with him, but he knew that he had to continue his life. Recounting the details that he had experienced while in his coma, John could not tear his reality from the dream. The detail was so vivid — the Cuillin Mountains, his life with Alex on the beautiful Isle of Skye. He recalled his meeting with Emanuel. "What did happen? It was all so real!" He told himself.

Several weeks passed, then months. His encounter did not diminish in his mind. Then he made a decision — as outlandish as it might seem — he had to try.

John sat at his desk and opened his laptop, where he held his fingers hovering over the keyboard for what seemed hours, then he did it. John typed...

Alex are you there?

There was a silence and nothing; the screen was blank.

John stood up, and he felt foolish about typing his stupid

note. Entering the kitchen, he made himself a mug of tea. He put two large spoons of sugar into it and began to stir. Lost in thought, he continued to stir. Suddenly he stopped. He heard a pinging sound of a message being delivered to his laptop. Gingerly, John returned to the desk. Breathing deeply he could barely look at the screen. "Oh just do it, it's probably work," he said to himself.

Sitting back in his seat at his desk, John gingerly looked at the screen. He saw the words...

I'm waiting for you.

***

John Ross did not remarry; although he did have a couple of casual, platonic relationships, they were never going to lead anywhere. He continued to work as a manager in several chains of restaurants; it was a job that he enjoyed, and it kept him in a comfortable but simple lifestyle. He never returned to the Highlands, that memory was too difficult for him. The memory of Alex, however, remained in the front of his mind until another forty-six years had passed.

John had enjoyed a quiet afternoon in his small but well-tended allotment where he had planted several row of leeks. He felt a little tired, and so he sat in an old but comfortable chair in his tiny shed. Here he closed his eyes, thinking of his beloved Alex.

John opened his eyes and found himself in a familiar place. He was standing in a tunnel, bright coloured lights surrounding him. He then saw a branch off to the left. Taking the turn, he followed it and found that it led to a viewing platform. He knew this place well. The lights around him appeared to be more intense this time. John did not have to think about what he was intended to do.

Looking through the portal, he could see a small croft house in the distance. It was home, and the front door was open.

This time, though, John knew that there was no barrier preventing him entering this dimension and so he simply stepped through. As he crossed the threshold, the age that he had gained in his birth realm vanished, and he was a young man again. Taking his first steps out of the portal onto the footpath, he was returning to the day he remembered so long ago, although it seemed like no time had ever passed. The footpath led John straight to the doorway that he knew so well, to the home he shared with his Alex.

Without a second thought, he entered and saw two glasses of fizz sitting on the kitchen table. Next to the glasses was the handwritten note he had left for Alex.

Then a door opened into the kitchen, and casually Alex walked through. She walked up to John and kissed him on the lips and said, "Great timing John, I was just preparing supper." She put her arms around him and said, "Listen to what's playing."

From a small radio sitting on the kitchen table music was playing softly. As they gently embraced, they began to dance. Alex whispered into John's ear, "By the way, Emanuel sends his regards."

They held each other tightly and smooched to *A lovers Concerto.*

A publication by Plan4 Publishing
For more information visit: plan4publishing.com

Artwork and layout by Plan4 Media
For more information visit: plan4media.com

For Tiger
For more information, please visit: www.rotjanashands.org